Lock Down Publications and Ca$h
Presents

I0666813

FO'EVA ROLLIN' 3

TOXIC LOVE

Written By
Assa Raymond Baker

First Edition 2024

Printed in the United States of America

Lock Down Publications
P.O. Box 944
Stockbridge, GA 30281
www.lockdownpublications.com

Like our page on Facebook: Lock Down Publications
www.facebook.com/lockdownpublications.ldp

Stay Connected with Us!

Text **LOCKDOWN** to 22828 to stay up-to-date with new releases, sneak peaks, contests and more…

Like our page on Facebook:
Lock Down Publications

Join Lock Down Publications/The New Era Reading Group

Visit our website:
www.lockdownpublications.com

Follow us on Instagram:
Lock Down Publications

Email Us: We want to hear from you!

Chapter 1

The crafty underboss, known to the underworld as Bomani, confidently slipped his large hands into a pair of black latex gloves before slamming a fully loaded magazine into the base of his M-4 rifle. He then replaced his simple black mask with a strategically chosen designer one. Unlike many others struggling to navigate in the crazy COVID-19 pandemic, Bomani and his team of outlaws loved being able to move with their faces hidden.

Okay, my plug call and hang up, I know what that mean / Give him 'bout twenty minutes / We'll rendezvous and he'll hit me off with them things / I play wholesale, I'm not breaking down, I got no use for no beam / But we wide open, my spot rollin' like a yo-yo with no string . . .

Head bobbing to the song *Pimp C 3000* by Starlito and Don Trip, the boss turned in his seat so he's facing his collaborators seated in the Durango with him, pleased to see everyone dressed to move.

"Sen, please keep in mind that we're going in here to break these fools, not to rack up a body count."

"Bro, I know the plan," Sen retorted, loudly exhaling and rolling her eyes at him.

"You can go'n with all that attitude! I'm just reminding you that we don't need none of yo' unnecessary bustin' this time," he said, checking his sister and giving her a scolding glare so she knows he's serious about what he said.

"Dawg, man, I told you that last wasn't on me," Sentrice said, as she pulled a designer roaring lion-printed mask up over her face.

On the heist that had Bomani cautioning Sentrice, a rent-a-cop tried to be a hero and save the day, but thanks to Sentrice's trigga happiness, that guard is now being remembered as a fallen hero.

" Shiesty, you ready to roll?" Bomani asked his man seated beside Sentrice in the backseat.

"Yeah, I'm good. I just had a long night," he answered, flashing a smile that did nothing to hide his hangover.

Shiesty must have seen the hint of suspicion in Bomani's hazel eyes because he promptly put on his green designer Hulk mask, then retrieved the two large duffle bags that he needed. Once inside, Shiesty's main job is to snatch as much product and money as he can carry, while Bomani and Sentrice keep the place secured.

"Ya better be," Bomani warned. "Say, DB, you keep this muthafucka running. The last thing we need is to come out that muthafucka blastin' and have to wait for yo' ass to start this bitch up."

"What, is this take-a-trip-down-fucked-up-memory-lane or some shit? I got this," DB promised, then unmuted the radio. He immediately lowered the volume and received a head nod from Bomani before he and the others hopped out and briskly approached the rear entrance of the illegal cannabis dispensary.

Chapter 2

Approximately 45 minutes before closing, the manager of a very lucrative vape shop that doubled as an underground cannabis dispensary arrived to collect the day's profit. As always, she was met at the door by a legally armed security guard.

"How you doing this evening, Tina?" the big husky security guard politely inquired as he held open the door for the manager of the dispensary to enter.

"I'm doing as well as one could be with that Corona virus out here like it is, just depopulating the world," she said, shaking her head. "I'll be glad when they make a vaccine available to us common folk."

"I hear you on that. You know them in the White House got one."

"How's that newborn of yours treating you?"

"He's good. I can't wait to hold him."

"Why haven't you held him yet?"

"Because I've been here dealing with a bunch of crazies who don't want to wear masks. I'm not trying to get either of them infected by accident, so I just stay away."

"OMG, Mark, how come you didn't ask for time off so you can be there for them?" Tina asked, surprised by the guard's sacrifice.

The loyal security guard of three years was about to answer, but the words froze in his throat when he saw a man wearing a Joker mask quickly approaching with an assault rifle trained on him. He didn't miss the other two masked armed men following close behind, also holding their guns at ready, daring him to make a move. The manager instantly began weeping as her and the guard were being forced into the building.

"All y'all get the fuck on the floor now!" Bomani barked, scaring everyone in the establishment. "Get face down with yo' hands where I can see 'em!" he ordered, slamming the guard's face down onto the floor, bloodying his nose before disarming him. Bomani also relieved him of his gun and handheld radio, quickly tossing it to Shiesty.

Sentrice aimed her two Glock 19s at the dispensary technicians standing with their hands held high behind the counter.

"We're good out here. Go, go!" Sentrice said, assuring Shiesty that they got everything under control.

With that, Shiesty tossed the terrified manager over the counter, promptly hurtling over it behind her. He then snatched her back to her feet by her blonde micro braids and slapped her into submission.

"Don't play dumb, bitch. Ya know what we here for, so take me to it now!" Shiesty aggressively insisted.

Fearing for her life, the manager didn't put up any resistance. She obediently led her captor to the vault room as she was directed.

"This is everything," she said once she'd put in the unlock security code. "But if you know what's good for you, you'll just leave now. Do you even know who this belongs to?" she asked, simultaneously pulling open the door.

"Bitch, shut up! It's mine now!" he barked, violently shoving her to the floor. Then Shiesty commenced filling up one of the two duffle bags with every cent he found in the safe. Once he had it all, he strapped that bag to his back and instantly went to filling up the other with product as quickly as he could. Shiesty abruptly stopped his looting when he heard over the radio that the silent alarm had been triggered.

"Oh, shit!" he swore, then grabbed the woman and rushed back up front to notify his team. "We got trouble! Somebody triggered the silent alarm!" he exclaimed when he got up front.

"Don't trip!" Bomani quickly glanced at his watch and found that they were making good time. Less than four minutes had passed since the time they entered the establishment. Behind his mask, he smiled with pride. "We still got like five minutes before anybody show up. So go back and grab as much as you can. I wanna be gone in two!" Bomani nonchalantly ordered.

"On it!" Shiesty said, then rushed back to the vault.

After witnessing the way the manager was being handled, the other women in the place began wailing.

"Stay calm, everybody, stay calm, and I promise nobody else gets hurt!" Bomani said, doing his best to keep everybody in line for the next few minutes so he and his team can finish what they'd started and get out of there.

Sentrice looked at the assistant manager and noticed the nervous look on her face.

"You're the one that hit that alarm, aren't you?" Sentrice asked her.

"I'm sorry!" she confessed with fresh tears streaming down her puffy face. "She told me to do it." She pointed to the woman beside her.

"Please don't hurt me. I have a fam—"

Sentrice put a bullet in the instigator's head before she could finish her sentence. Then she turned her gun on the assistant manager and shot her as well. Before her body hit the floor, Sentrice was already squeezing off on the screaming manager.

"Make sho y'all on point!" Bomani shouted after seeing his sister spatter the manager's thoughts on the wall behind her. "Time to bounce!" he yelled when he saw Shiesty emerge from the back with both duffle bags filled and strapped over his shoulders.

Without being told, Sentrice briskly marched towards the exit to make sure the coast was clear in the front, while her fuming brother covered their backs. Once outside, the trio quickly hopped in the waiting getaway vehicle. Before every door had shut on the Durango, DB was stomping on the gas pedal. The powerful supercharged Hemi engine burned the tires, leaving smoking skid marks in the alley behind the illegal dispensary.

The team sat deathly quiet as the truck stormed down city blocks, until DB felt they were far enough away to slow to the posted speed limit. Not long after reducing speed, DB whipped the Durango into a parking garage where the others had their personal vehicles stashed waiting for their return.

All four of them hopped out of the truck when it stopped. Steaming mad, Bomani snatched his mask from his face and grabbed one of the duffle bags, while Shiesty removed his and grabbed the other bag. Sentrice immediately stomped off, not removing her mask until she got in her antique gold Mustang. Without her help, DB swapped out the bogus plates and peeled off the fake decals running down both sides of his truck. The others helped before getting into their own cars.

"Aye, y'all meet me at the spot in like an hour!" Bomani instructed, changing out of his colorful laughing Joker half-mask as he tossed the bags on his backseat, then climbed in the driver seat, immediately igniting the engine.

They all agreed. The Durango was the first to depart from the parking garage, followed by Shiesty's gray Ford F-150, Bomani's cream Impala, and lastly Sentrice's Mustang.

Chapter 3

Immediately upon entering her crime scene through the front entrance, Detective Tonya Lont observed bodies and blood spatter where the gunshot victims lay. She stepped over to where the deceased were being photographed and examined by the crime scene investigative team.

"Detective Lont?" a uniformed officer standing nearby inquired.

"Yes."

"Detective Hermon is waiting for you in the back by the vault."

"Okay, where is that?"

"Once you go through that door, you can't miss it," he informed her as he pointed in the direction of the vault.

"Thank you!" Lont said, then walked off, taking in every bit of the scene as she headed to where she'd been told to go.

"Tonya! Over here!" Hermon yelled, calling Lont over to where he stood viewing surveillance video of the robbery homicide.

"What did I miss?" she asked once she was standing beside her fellow detective.

"I'll start it over so we can swap theories over coffee," he said, restarting the video and stepping out of her way.

The first thing that stood out to Lont was the organization of the trio. She watched as they moved as one, leaving the security guard no chance to react in any way that would prevent his immediate death. They forced the guard and the woman through the open door leading inside the building.

"Do you know who the female is?" Lont asked without looking away from the screen.

"She's the manager and the owner's girlfriend," Hermon answered.

In the video, Lont noticed that one of the robbers went right for the manager, who was the key to opening the safe. This told her that the robbers had done their homework because they knew exactly who to go after. The detective watched on as one of the masked men tossed the terrified manager over the counter before hopping over it behind her. The forceful manner in which the robber snatched her back to her feet told Lont that he knew her.

Fearing for her life, the manager didn't put up any further resistance. She obediently led the masked man to the vault room. Then the video flipped again, showing a view of the lobby. This is where the detective wished the video had audio, because, all of a sudden, one of the robbers raised his gun and shot a clerk in the head, then continued killing the employees but no one else. That action made Lont very curious.

After watching the video, Lont followed Hermon outside where they began questioning the people who were inside the building at the time of the robbery homicide. No one knew anything more than what the video had shown, or they were too shaken up to be of help to the detectives at the time. That's when Lont decided to have another chat with the owner of the smoke shop.

On her approach, she observed a man briskly walking away from where the owner stood. She knew that whoever it was didn't want to be questioned by her. She assumed the man had warrants he was avoiding being captured for. His departure also made the detective suspect that a few more bodies would be dropping behind the death of the owner's wife. Lont made a mental note to inquire further when she spoke to the owner this second time.

Chapter 4

Jaheim pulled up to the scene out front of his friend Chief Monty's smoke shop and could immediately tell by how many police and press vehicles were parked helter-skelter out front that whatever had happened inside wasn't good. It was a flashing light show in every direction he looked.

"Why in the fuck did he call me to this bitch with all this shit going on out here?" Jaheim asked himself aloud as he got out of his car.

A large crowd of news reporters and neighborhood folk hovered along the outskirts of the yellow police barrier, all buzzing with speculations of what happened inside. Jaheim zigzagged and pushed his way through them, heading towards the building. He ducked under the yellow tape and was immediately stopped by a white uniformed officer clutching his weapon.

"Back under the tape now!" the officer yelled. "This is a crime scene here, and unless you're itching to become our prime suspect, I suggest you get back on the other side and don't cross it again!"

"Fuck you! My brother and sister own this place. He's the one that called me down here. Do you want me to call him so you can ask him yourself?" Jaheim retorted, putting on the act of grief-stricken family member.

"I'm sorry about that, sir, but I can't allow you inside," the officer apologized. "But sir, I was told to have all of the family members to wait over by that gold detective cruiser," he said, allowing him to remain inside the tape and pointing him in the direction of the waiting area.

Jaheim nodded, then proceeded over to where he spotted his big homie standing with an evil frown on his face.

"CM! What happened?"

"Nothing good, nothing good at all. They killed my BM!" responded the distraught business owner and gang chief. "This is the second time them fuckers hit me in almost two months!" he fumed.

"You sure it's the same crew?" Jaheim inquired as he scrutinized the men surrounding his big homie. With that piece of information, his mind instantly fixed on it being someone close to him—it might be an inside job.

"Positive!" Chief Monty barked. "Jah, right now you're the only nigga I trust. I need you to find 'em and handle 'em!"

"CM, are you sure you want me on this?" Jaheim questioned, because the last time Chief Monty hired him to do something, innocent people were killed in the shootout and chase that went down on that mission. The big man didn't like the way Jaheim had gone about it because his recklessness had almost caused a war with the E.S.G. (East Side Gangsterz).

"Jah, fuck that past shit! This here is different. Them muthafuckas killed the mother of my kids," Chief Monty said with tears frozen in the wells of his eyes. "Name your price. I don't care, just make 'em pay for taking her from us!"

"Say less. I got you," he assured the big homie.

Jaheim had heard about a series of big-money robberies that had taken place around the city over the last few months. The majority of the rumors said three violent gunmen walked into a spot and stripped it, always shooting or killing at least one person each time.

"What got you convinced that it's the same people?"

"I got 'em both on video."

"You got both of what on video?"

"The first robbery and this one. I've already watched the whole thing."

"I need to see 'em."

"I know but I can't watch it again. I'm just gonna send it to yo' phone." Chief Monty walked over to his personal bodyguard, retrieved his phone, and forwarded Jaheim the video. "That's the one from in there right now." Chief Monty fumed.

Jaheim turned his back to him and the bodyguard while he carefully studied the video sent to his phone. He was looking for anything that might give him a lead. The first thing he noticed was the trio weren't afraid to use their weapons. Also in the video, he noticed that one of the robbers went straight to the woman who had the key to the safe, which meant they had done their homework—or it was an inside job, so they knew exactly who to go after. He also noticed that the trio didn't stay inside for very long either.

Jaheim suspected that the one who kept checking his watch was the leader. Whoever this stickup crew was, they were very clever in the way they used their matching caps and masks. They knew that anyone close enough to see them would only remember their characters but nothing about them.

"Hold on, what's this?" Jaheim whispered to himself. Talking to himself was one of the habits he'd picked up during the heavy years he'd spent locked up in solitary confinement as a juvenile. "Back it up, back it up," he sang, rewinding the video a few seconds and pressing play. Jaheim noticed from the way one of them moved that one of the robbers was a female—or a very feminine man.

"Aye, big homie, I know you said you don't wanna look at this nomo, but one of 'em is a girl and I need you to tell me if you know this chick." Jaheim explained, holding out the phone to him.

"How can you be sure?" Chief Monty asked.

"Look at that ass and the way she stands. That's a girl all day. If not, it's what I'm running with for now," Jaheim said, resisting a smile.

"Yeah, that's a woman," Chief Monty and his bodyguard both agreed. "But without a clear shot of her face I don't know the bitch."

"Say nomo. Here come that detective bitch Lont again," the bodyguard alerted them.

"Aye, I don't need to be questioned, so I'm out. I need to see them other videos though. I might be able to pick her out from one of 'em."

"I'll send 'em to your phone as soon as I can get to my laptop," Chief Monty promised.

Jaheim made his exit before he could be questioned by the nosey MPD homicide detective. He zigzagged his way back through the crowd and hopped back in his ocean-blue and gunmetal- painted Dodge Hellcat. Unable to resist, he made sure to make the tires squeal as a middle finger to the cops while he cruised away.

Chapter 5

Bomani ordering a meeting after a job wasn't out of the norm. It's something he'd always done to split up the loot. What worried Sentrice was the look in her big brother's eyes when he called it. The way Bomani stared at her told her that if she wasn't his sister, he would've killed her without a second thought. Now she sat in her car at the corner of 76th and Brown Deer Road, trying to run from her thoughts at the stoplight.

I might slap the shit out a bitch, caught her playin' around (playin' around) / I rock Prada, fuck with ballers that be movin' pounds (trappers) / Make that nigga ice me out, these hoes gon' fuck for free though (free though) / I get chips like Cheetos, 1942, no Tito (nah) / Bitch, I'm quarantine clean, you can't touch me with gloves / Nigga rollin' off a bean, tryna shoot up the club (shoot up the club) / Hate when silly hoes talk crazy on the 'Gram, bitch, get your bag up / I'm a city girl with the backend, can't wait to go and act up.

Sentrice rapped along to her favorite song by Mulatto and 21 Savage, which hummed through the custom sound system of her Mustang.

Sentrice wasn't always so cold-hearted and possessive of her brother. A few tragic situations that occurred in her life as a child had made her this way. The main tragedy was losing both of her parents in a car accident. After that, she didn't care whether she lived or died. On her 16th birthday, she attempted suicide by overdose. It was Bomani who found her passed out on the floor of her bedroom, clutching a happy family photo of them. From that day on, her bond with her brother became unbreakable. Bomani was strict on her, but she knew it was only because he wanted the best for her.

Lowering the volume of her car stereo, Sentrice turned into the South Lawn housing project's parking lot. She whipped into the first open slot she came to and hopped out. Sentrice took deep breaths with every step as she ambled up to and entered the house that Bomani used as their weapons storage spot and for planning jobs. Other than that, no one lived in the place.

"Bomani, I heard what you said to me before we went in there, but—"

"Sen, sit yo' hothead ass down!" Bomani's voice boomed, cutting her off mid-sentence.

She shut up and took a seat on the sofa beside Shiesty. Then her brother commenced scolding her in front of everybody.

"What's next for us?" Sentrice asked, pretending she didn't care about the tongue-lashing she'd just gotten. But everyone could see she was in a worse mood. Her feelings were hurt, but she hid it the best she could by trying to keep a neutral face.

Bomani smiled for the first time since Sentrice walked through the door.

"I feel we need to change things up a bit. Especially after what happened," he said, glaring at Sentrice, who rolled her eyes at him the way she always did after they got into an argument or whatever. "So I'm thinking we should hit that wannabe El Chapo's shit next."

"Whoa! Are you serious?" DB asked, almost choking on his beer.

"Yep, I'm as serious as all this fresh cash sitting between us," Bomani answered, shifting his loyal soldiers' attention off of him and his sister's family drama and onto the neat piles of cash on the coffee table.

"Dawg, man, I don't give a fuck. You know if you say we doing it, I'm wit' it. Just give me a coupla days to make love to that," Shiesty said, pointing to the money.

"Ugh! Don't you mean so you can lose it paying a bitch to make love to you?" Sentrice teased him, as she always did whenever they got together.

"Hater!" he smiled. "Sen, you know that don't look good on you. All ya gotta do is loosen up, and then maybe you'll find a nigga to spend some bread on yo' ugly ass for once in yo' life," he retorted.

"Ugly? Nigga, you wish you could get close enough to smell a bitch as fine as me!" she shot back with a flip of her hair.

"Aye, aye! If y'all done, I wanna hear more," DB exclaimed, laughing while trying to put things back on track.

Sentrice and Shiesty settled down after having a short pillow fight. Bomani joined in on the fight and the laughter before continuing.

"We're going to catch 'em when they make their last pickup for the day. I've been scoping out their last drop-off, because that's when they'll have nothin' but that paper on 'em," Bomani explained.

"Sound like a plan to me," DB agreed.

"The niggaz doin' the transport are trained to go, so when we hitting 'em, we're gonna have to body one or two of 'em," Bomani said, glancing over at Sentrice.

"Don't be looking at me like that!" she exclaimed, grinning. "I'm retired. All I'm doing from now on is driving. DB can have my spot."

"Liar!" the men exclaimed in unison, all bursting with laughter.

After the meeting was over, Sentrice hopped in her car and sped away from the house. She merged onto the highway and just drove. Whenever she needed to escape or think less, the highway was her answer. It was something about driving while listening to calm R&B music that relaxed her mind and put her at ease.

During her ride, Bomani's scolding words replayed repeatedly in her head:

"We're not hittin' these licks for a fuckin' reputation! We're takin' 'em down so we can get paid! Sen, you should know that the more bodies you drop, the harder muthafuckas are gonna be gunning for us. And instead of us being able to just walk in and takin' what we want and skippin' out, it'll be a fuckin' war zone every muthafuckin' time!"

With hurt feelings, Sentrice pressed on the gas, turned up the radio, and zoned out as she sailed down the freeway.

Chapter 6

Jaheim pretty much just twisted aimlessly through the city banging his *Street Nigga Music* playlist while sipping from a leftover bottle of Crown Royal that he'd found in his glove compartment. He thought about what happened at Chief Monty's. All that was on his mind was tracking down the ones responsible for his big homie's pain and making them pay. With all he had to go on being what he'd seen in the video, Jaheim knew making them pay wouldn't be easy.

Jaheim had just pulled up in front of Mia's. She's a friend with benefits who'd just posted photos of the baked barbecue chicken dinner she'd finished cooking. Since he was now a little tipsy and hungry as a hostage, he schemed to raid her kitchen and then bend her over for a quickie before getting back on his grind.

Jaheim was just about to step out of the car when his cellphone rang, playing his elderly Aunt Faye's ringtone. His Aunt Faye was one of the few people in his life whose calls he couldn't ignore.

"Hello, Auntie!"

"Jah-jah, is you here?"

"Yes, ma'am, if you're askin' if I'm in the city."

"Okay, then go over by LaQuess's and see what is going on over there. I'm worried because we were talking on the phone and got cut off, and now she's not answering her cell or house phone. I think that punk James is over there fighting her because she got tired of him cheating on her and put his sorry tail out earlier," Aunt Faye explained.

"I'm not far from her place now, so I'm on my way. I'll have her call you when I find out what's goin' on."

"Jah-jah, kick his ass if he put his hands on my baby. You hear me?"

"Yes, ma'am. I'll handle it," he promised before ending the call.

Jaheim usually didn't get involved in domestic situations because most of the time, they ended up right back together the same day, if not a few days later. But this was different because his aunt knows not to call him if she really didn't want to happen what he would go over there and do. So, he slammed his car door back and sent Mia a text telling her he'd be right back and asking her to keep everything warm for him.

Roughly five minutes later, Jaheim pulled to a stop on 20th and Highland, in front of his cousin's apartment building. He placed his gun on his waist, concealing it beneath his shirt, before hopping out of the car and entering the building. Rather than wait for the slow elevator, Jaheim decided to dash up the two flights of stairs.

Stepping into the second-floor hallway, he briskly marched down to LaQuess's door. He took a moment to listen for anything that sounded like trouble going on inside. He could faintly hear his cousin telling someone to leave her alone. With that, Jaheim politely knocked firmly on the door.

"Who dat?" A deep male voice bellowed, answering the knock.

"Is Quess here?" Jaheim asked, knowing the curiosity of a man asking for her after she'd put him out would make ole James open the door. And just as expected, a few moments later, Jaheim heard the locks being flipped, and then a tall biracial man peeked out of the door.

"Yeah, whud up? Who you?" asked the tall biracial man with a strong Spanish accent.

"Quess's mother sent me over here to check on her, so can you call her to the door, please?" Jaheim said, avoiding the man's inquiry.

"Nawl, she good—you can leave!" the man said, then attempted to shut the door.

Jaheim quickly stuck his foot in the doorway before he could close it. Though he'd never seen James before, Jaheim noticed fresh scratches on the man's neck and shoulder that pretty much confirmed his aunt's suspicions as well as his identity.

"I said I need to see her!" Jaheim said, pushing back on the door.

"Alright, okay—you can see her," James conceded with a bit of a sinister tone as he stepped aside. Jaheim stepped foot inside the apartment, immediately noticing that the place was a mess, clearly from them scuffling. There were clothes hanging out of white trash bags piled beside the door, with broken glass and furniture lying in clear view.

"There she goes, nigga. Ya happy now?" James stated, standing off to the side behind him.

Jaheim looked at his cousin sitting on the couch, right away noticing a few droplets of blood at her feet along with bruises on the side of her face and neck.

"Cuz, yo' mama sent me to make sure you're okay."

"Now look what he did to my face, Jah!" LaQuess cried as she pulled her hair back and fully faced him.

"What do you want me to do?" he asked angrily, staring down James and preparing to issue the beating his aunt told him to give, no matter what LaQuess's answer was.

"Say, nigga, whud you mean by dat?" James barked.

"Fuck him, Jah! Beat his ass!" she answered.

As soon as Jaheim took a step toward James, the coward leaped out into the hallway, making a foolish dash for the elevator. Jaheim gave chase, quickly catching him. He shoved James hard, causing him to crash into the hard metal elevator doors, then immediately began pounding on his face. Somehow James managed to get to his feet. The punch-drunk punk tried to turn his back, shielding his face. Without missing a step, Jaheim grabbed him up in a tight bear hug. James savagely threw back an elbow that connected with Jaheim's forehead. The unexpected blow dazed Jaheim a little, allowing James a chance to break free of the hold and throw a wild right fist, landing four times in Jaheim's face.

The tall man staggered but was able to slam his size 13 foot into Jaheim's midsection. The kick doubled him over. Seeing this, James quickly took advantage by placing a tight chokehold on Jaheim.

"That's right, muthafucka—go to sleep!" James growled, applying more pressure to the hold on his neck.

Jaheim fought hard to break free of the hold. He slammed his elbow violently back into James's ribs, fracturing them. James instantly released him, allowing Jaheim to catch his breath and steady himself. Good again, Jaheim pounced, taking him to the floor and commencing to deliver a savage ground-and-pound to James's face, knocking him unconscious.

Suddenly, out of nowhere, LaQuess rushed over and began kicking the defenseless man in the head and face.

"You bitch! You bitch! You bitch!" she screamed with every merciless blow. Then she pressed Jaheim's gun that he'd dropped while tussling with James to her ex-boyfriend's temple.

"Quess!" Jaheim shouted, snapping her out of her madness. "Stop! You don't wanna do that," he said, carefully removing the gun from her trembling hands and then hugging her tightly. "Go get your stuff so I can take you to your mother's," he told her as he walked her back to her apartment.

"No! I'm not runnin' from that punk!" she retorted, abruptly stopping at the door and taking a good look at the mess her tussling with James inside the cozy one-bedroom apartment had made.

"I know. Runnin' isn't in our bloodline, so I'll never suggest that. I just don't want you here alone tonight—that's all."

"Okay, since you don't want me here alone, can you take me to my friend's bar? I'll stay with him tonight and come clean this up later."

"Okay, boyfriend number two it is," he teased, making her smile. "Go get ready while I drag that trash-ass nigga outside," Jaheim told her after seeing one of her nosy neighbors peek out of their apartment.

LaQuess agreed, then headed toward her bedroom, leaving him to handle his business. Jaheim marched back over to the unconscious ex, rolled him into the elevator, drew his gun, and climbed in with him. Jaheim was not only going to escort James out—he was also going to make sure that he didn't bother LaQuess again.

Chapter 7

Sentrice knew the points her big brother made were right, but she still felt the moves she'd made in their last job were justified. News of the deadly robbery was all over the TV and social media. The major news outlets were describing them as armed and dangerous, just like Bomani said they would, and still, she felt she made the right choices.

After driving around for over an hour, Sentrice came across a nice, low-key-looking nightclub named *Savoy*. She usually didn't go out to unknown places alone, but after the tongue-lashing she received from her brother, she really didn't feel like having any of them in her face.

She circled the block, then decided that *Savoy* might be the escape she was craving. She stopped and read a sign on the door informing all that it was open mic night. The place offered drinks, music, and laughter. Sentrice was sold, knowing that she needed all three of those things. She parked, exited the car, and headed toward the entrance of the nightclub where a big bouncer stood waiting. The sight of the bulldog-looking bouncer made her feel at ease about having to leave her gun in the car.

"Spread your arms and turn around!" the bouncer said with authority, looking like he couldn't wait to thoroughly frisk her.

Sentrice was used to men making passes at her and doing whatever to get their hands on her well-built 160 lbs., 5'7" frame. Shiesty once described her as a darker-complexion

Megan Thee Stallion, but she didn't see the comparison in the mirror—nor did Sentrice think she was darker than her. All Sentrice ever saw was a gangsta bitch staring back at her.

"Big boy, I know you can see that I'm not hiding anything, so if you touch me, I'ma hit you where it hurts!" Sentrice warned him.

"Damn! It's like that, sweety?" he said, raising his hands in surrender.

"Sweety, it's all hands-free here until it's not. And then I promise you—you really don't wanna feel my hands on you then. But before you go in, I gotta wave you through."

Sentrice allowed him to run the handheld metal detector over her body and was permitted inside unmolested. She sat at the bar, relaxing as she sipped on her iced Patron, trying her best not to make eye contact with a sexy guy seated at the far end of the bar. She wasn't dressed for a night out clubbing but still wore her navy blue Prada pantsuit and gold Prada wedge sandals. Her neck-length rose-brown hair had been tied back with the help of her rearview mirror, leaving the sides loose so they framed her face. Sentrice knew she didn't look bad, but she wasn't at her best to be meeting someone new.

"Waiting or escaping?"

"What?" Sentrice questioned, looking away from the TV mounted in the corner above the bar. She found the handsome stranger from the end of the bar had crept up on her. The vibe he gave off caused her blood to warm and rush.

"I'm just wondering why a woman as sexy as you is sitting at the bar? I figure you're either waiting on someone to arrive or escaping from a bad day," he explained.

"Oh," Sentrice smiled. "I'm definitely escaping."

"I knew it. Dare if I sit and escape with you? The drinks will be cheaper!"

"How can I say no to that?" she answered, watching him sit on the open stool beside her.

"See, you're 'bout ready for a refill. I'm a man of my word, so let me handle that for you," he said, waving to the bartender without taking his eyes off her.

"I was always warned not to drink with strangers, soooo?"

"Jaheim—but most call me Jah. I'm already knowing I'ma like hearing either one roll off your tongue," he flirted.

"Be careful what you wish for. I'm known to be a bit of a potty mouth," she flirted back.

"That makes two of us. Do I get to know yours, or do I come up with my own name for you?"

"Noooo, that's not sexy. I had that happen to me once before, and things didn't end well. My name's Sen. It's short like yours, but I prefer Sen, so let's leave it at that."

"It's left," Jaheim said, then heard the club DJ call LaQuess to the stage. "What the fuck is this girl on now?" He instantly stood and faced the stage.

"What is it?" Sentrice asked, standing as well.

"It's my cousin. She's escaping from a helluva day herself. Come on, let's go see this up close." Jaheim grabbed her by the hand, and she grabbed her drink and willingly let him lead her to an open table right in front of the stage.

"Heeeeyy, Cuzo!" a very tipsy LaQuess exclaimed from up on center stage. As soon as her eyes fell on Sentrice, she said, "Daaaamn, Jah, you move fast. A bitch turned up her glass, and you done went and caught a new bitch before I can even swallow!" LaQuess couldn't help but giggle at herself. "How you doin', gurl?"

"Not as good as you. Yet!" Sentrice answered, raising her glass to LaQuess in salute, then gulping down the shot.

"I ain't gonna lie, bitch—you sho look guuuud. I . . . I used to look as good as you. Dat was befo' I woke my dumbass up and realized the nigga I was fuckin' with wasn't shit! You—you know what, ladies? I'm gonna sing it out and want all my bitches to sing this song with me," LaQuess said, then waved to the DJ.

Moments later, LaQuess started singing, and it was clear to Sentrice and everyone else that she was no comedian. LaQuess had almost every couple in the house up on their feet, with the women singing Mary J. Blige's song, *Not Gon' Cry,* with her. Jaheim didn't pass on the chance to pull Sentrice close. The soulfulness of LaQuess's voice, laced with being wrapped in a pair of warm, protective arms, gave Sentrice goosebumps.

Everything in the moment felt so right. Even after the crowd around Sentrice and Jaheim gave LaQuess a warm, exciting round of applause, the two continued swaying in each other's arms right into the next song. Somewhere halfway through *I Can't Stop Loving You* by Kem, Jaheim's lips found their way onto Sentrice's neck. He floated tiny kisses in a half-circle, and she melted deeper into his arm. The foreplay instantly went back and forth, and by the end of the set, they both walked off the dance floor knowing they wouldn't be going home alone.

Chapter 8

Bomani stood 6'3", approximately 200 lbs, casually dressed in a tailored white silk Armani button-up shirt, gray slacks with thin white pinstripes, and gray-and-white snakeskin loafers trimmed with soft leather. He was carrying a large black leather shoulder bag over his broad shoulder, looking like he'd stepped out of a movie set. Bomani's long stride oozed a sexy confidence that turned the heads of both sexes as he walked by.

The fearless outlaw ambled through the lobby of the Chicago Museum of Art, dressed to impress as always. But unlike usual, Bomani's mind wasn't completely on handling the business that brought him to the Windy City. He couldn't stop thinking about how heartless his baby sister had become over the last few months. What troubled him most was the fact that he had nobody to blame for it but himself. He had allowed Sentrice into his lifestyle instead of insisting that she go off to school, the way their long-deceased parents had planned for them both.

From Sentrice's actions in the last robbery, Bomani knew it was time for a major change in their lives. This is why, immediately after having the team meeting concerning her actions during the robbery, he rushed home, quickly showered, changed into the outfit he was wearing, then jumped back into his car and drove down to Chicago to meet with a suave financial investor named Eric Nash. Eric was the president of Shoreline Investments, and Bomani chose to meet with him because Nash was rumored to be the man to see if you had a lot of dirty money and were looking to clean it up.

Bomani was snapped out of his thoughts by a text message notifying him that his ride was outside waiting for him. He promptly exited the museum and slid into the back seat of the black Cadillac Escalade that Mr. Nash had sent for him. Bomani knew he was stepping into the big leagues by the fully stocked mini bar in the back of the luxurious SUV. Once seated, the driver informed him that the bar was open to him. Bomani helped himself to a stiff drink and, just to be on the safe side, insisted that the driver have one as well. Bomani knew that if this was a setup by law enforcement, an undercover officer wouldn't drink and drive. The driver not only accepted the drink but asked him to make his a double.

During the lengthy ride across the Windy City, Bomani stared blankly out the window, his and his sister's futures on his mind. He knew if everything with their next job went smoothly, they'd finally be able to retire. Securing their future was the loving big brother's sole purpose for scheduling the meeting with Mr. Nash. Since he'd been forced into manhood by the deaths of his parents, Bomani had been playing a mental game of chess with his life. He strategically set up all the right moves so that once it was all over, he and Sentrice would be able to retire from the real-life game of cops and robbers without having any real financial worries. He chose to only rob illegally run businesses.

The SUV turned onto the driveway of a big, luxurious home and parked. The driver got out and opened the back door for Bomani. He quickly downed the rest of his drink before stepping out of the truck and approaching the front door of the home, where he was greeted by Mr. Nash himself.

"Terrible with names, so please correct me if I'm mispronouncing yours, Mr. Boomanniel?"

"Close—it's Bo-mani without the E-L, but you can just call me Bo," Bomani said, extending his hand to the shorter, heavyset man.

"Great, it's a pleasure to meet you, Bo. You can call me Eric," he said, giving Bomani's hand a firm shake. "How was the drive here? I instructed my driver to take the scenic route."

"It was nice. I've never been to this part of Chicago."

"Most haven't. What parts have you visited?"

"Just downtown and some of the inner South and West Sides," Bomani answered, following Eric into the mini mansion.

"That figures. I hope after we're done here you don't have to rush back home right away. I'd like to show you the fun parts of the city."

"Let's see how things go with this, and I'll let you know," Bomani replied, not missing the quick flirtatious wink Eric tossed his way.

"Smart thinking!" Eric replied, entering a nicely sized, beautifully decorated office complete with a sitting area and a cozy fireplace.

"You have a nice home. This is the way I see myself living in the near future," Bomani complimented as Eric sat down in plush leather chairs in front of the fireplace.

Moments later, a woman who looked like she could've been a runway model entered the room carrying two snifters of Crown Royal Black in her hands.

"Bo, this is my lovely wife, Kerri," Eric said, making introductions as she handed each of them drinks.

"I was just telling your husband that you have a nice home here," Bomani said as he shook her soft, slender hand and accepted the iced brandy.

"Thanks, I'm glad someone likes my taste," she said, giving her husband a wink before leaving the room.

"Let's get to why I requested to meet with you, and thank you for making time for me after work hours," Bomani said once they were alone again.

"It's nothing. Many of my clients prefer not to meet in the office," Eric admitted, then took a sip of his drink.

"I have a nice sum of cash sitting around that needs a job," Bomani said as he removed his mask, judging they were a safe distance apart. "I'm looking to clean it up and invest it in something that'll have me and mine set. I've been told that you're the man to make it happen," he said, then took a sip himself.

Bomani was looking to invest a total of two million dollars, which was pretty much all the money he and Sentrice had stashed, so he had to be sure everything Eric said was legit.

"You haven't been told anything wrong. I can assure you, Bo, that I'm your man," Eric smiled. "My team and I will tailor an investment plan where your money can sit and gain the interest you desire and then some," Eric said with confidence, downing the rest of his drink in one gulp.

"I'm sure that you're good at what you do, especially living like this. But I have to ask you—what's the risk? Because I'm going to be trusting you with all my life savings. I had to work extremely hard to get this money, so I just want to be sure everything will work out like you say it will," Bomani said, sipping his drink.

"Bo, I had this very same conversation with R. Kelly before he went in. Like I told him, I can assure you that you have nothing to worry about. Every month, you will receive an account statement updating you on what's going on with your investment, and if we see anything that looks like it will slide the other way, we will pull out, reinvest it elsewhere, and keep it stacking. With my plan, there is no risk of you losing everything. But for appearances, every now and then, I will have to accept small losses, though nothing that will affect your primary investment."

"What's in it for you?" Bomani asked, taking another sip of his drink, liking what he was hearing.

"For the type of service you're requesting, the cost is 20% for the first year of your investment."

"Can you do 15%?" Bomani countered.

"No, I'm afraid that price is non-negotiable," Eric said firmly, then asked, "How much will you be investing with us at Shoreline?"

"Two mill," Bomani answered proudly.

"Two million is a very nice place for us to get started on building you the financial freedom you're looking for. And with an investment that large, the 20% fee won't faze you," Eric said with a greedy grin. "Bo, I don't have any problem with you going home and sleeping on it and getting back to me when you're ready."

"I'm ready now," Bomani said, simultaneously sliding the bag he'd sat beside the chair in front of them and unzipping it so Eric could observe the two million in neatly banded cash inside. "I don't like making blank trips, and I never go into anything without researching it first. I had my mind made up about investing with you long before now." Bomani made sure Eric was looking at him when he told him the money in front of them was his life savings again. "Eric, I'm trusting you to do all that you just said you can do for me. Please don't disappoint me."

"Bo, you're in good hands. As an added bonus, I'll personally insure 50% of your investment out of my own pocket. It's no secret that I hate losing money, especially my money. Trust me—you're in good hands."

With that assurance, Bomani sealed the deal with a firm handshake and another drink, this time with Eric and his lovely wife.

Chapter 9

Jaheim and Sentrice made their way from the dance floor to the bar, both feeling the need for a drink. They continued talking and flirting in between slamming shot after shot. The two shared an unspoken plan to get wasted and blame everything that happened afterward on their intoxication.

"It's about to be last call, and I'm not through with you," Jaheim said, slamming his last shot of tequila.

"Sooo, what's next? No, no, better yet—your place or mine?" she asked, giving him a smile that spoke louder than words.

A short time after leaving the club, Sentrice found herself pinned against the door of her home, with Jaheim's hands and lips all over her. The moment she felt his strong hands touch her bare skin, shockwaves shot through her, and the way he sucked her neck sent her past the point of no return. It had been two months since Sentrice had been with anyone like this. From the way Jaheim was touching her, she knew giving herself to him after going so long without wasn't going to be a letdown. She let his soft lips wander down her neck while her slender hands worked on undoing his pants. Once inside his jeans, she reached around and grabbed his behind, pulling him tightly to her. Sentrice melted even more just from the feeling of his long, warm, hard length pressing against her belly.

Jaheim felt shiver after shiver shooting through the beauty's body. Each one told him that his touch was warming his sweet destination down between her sexy thighs. He pulled her top off and allowed her to do the same to him as he followed her into her bedroom, leaving a trail of clothing along the way. Now skin to skin, with everything inside of them burning with a shared desire, Jaheim pushed her down on the bed and dragged her pants off her wide hips.

Sentrice wiggled to help him out, then just as eagerly peeled him out of his boxers while he popped the clasps of her lacy, flesh-colored bra. As soon as his mouth covered her nipple, the feeling made tiny explosions go off deep in her belly. And when Jaheim dropped down between her legs and began brushing his firm tongue over her cleanly shaved box, her moans filled the air. Using two of his thick fingers, he parted her lower lips while almost simultaneously snaking his tongue between them to dance with her clit. Jaheim was loving the feeling of her wetness against his chin as she came for him.

Sentrice was trying to catch her breath when she felt his tip slipping into her mouth. Without protest or hesitation, she started sucking and licking his hardness from his sack to his tip, loving every long inch. Impressed with his size, she pushed him away.

"Jah, I need to feel you in me. Fuck me, baby," she encouraged him by pulling her legs behind her head.

Jaheim released a lustful growl as he commenced pounding her out—hard and fast, shallow and deep—for a full two minutes. Then he flipped her over onto her stomach, dragged her partway off the bed, and slammed back into her wetness from the back, nice and hard, just the way she was begging him to. A few short minutes later, Sentrice felt Jaheim filling her box with his warm seed. He came back to back, then collapsed beside her.

Chapter 10

Outside in the gloomy alley behind a known underground uptown gambling house, Shiesty was preparing to start a fight with two guys he thought had cheated him in a craps game where he had lost approximately $100,000 in cash. While Shiesty ranted and raved at the top of his lungs, one of the alleged cheaters picked up a two-inch by four-foot block of wood that was being used as a security beam for the door and was about to clobber Shiesty upside his head with it when a scantily dressed female intervened, saving his very intoxicated self from what was sure to be a royal thrashing.

"Hey, hey, y'all! He's with me. Anyways, Phat Bastard lookin' for y'all upstairs," said the female, dressed in what looked to Shiesty like a Swiss-cheesed halter top and a tan leather handkerchief that was being worn as a mini skirt.

"Fuck that, Lil Mama! You ain't gotta stop 'em!" Shiesty exclaimed, slurring his words as he stood in an awkward fighting stance.

"Baby, do you really wanna be rolling around in the dirt fightin' them, or rolling in the bed with me?" the girl asked, trying her best to persuade him to let the alleged infraction go. "Don't let them ruin our night," she said, intertwining her arm with his.

Giving in to the beauty and his lust, Shiesty led her to his car after the guys went back inside the house. The girl looked at him as if he'd lost his mind when he went to open the driver's door of his car.

"I'm not lettin' you drive us no place drunk as you are right now!"

"Can you drive then?" he inquired.

"Yeah, but I rode with someone here. I'll call us an Uber."

"Fuck that! Here, drive my shit, 'cuz I ain't leavin' it here so them punks can strip my shit or some shit," Shiesty said, tossing her his keys. "You fo'real 'bout lettin' a nigga smash, right?"

"Hell, yeah! I want you to beat this pussy up. I know a motel not far from here where we can get a cheap room for the night . . ."

"Ma, I don't do motels, especially not cheap ones," Shiesty said, shaking his head. "We goin' to my crib so I can give you the time of yo' life," he suggested, then laid his head back on the headrest.

"You sure that'll be cool?" she asked. "I'm tryna get fucked good. I don't have time to be fightin' off no crazy girlfriend 'bout you."

"I don't have one of those, yet. I live by my damn. It's just gon' be the two of us—unless you wanna pick up a friend?" he said, smiling.

"You need to show me that you can handle this here first before anything like that go down," she retorted.

Shiesty gave her directions to his place, and during the drive, she told him her name was Aryana. They made small talk, flirting the entire way, until they pulled up in front of a soft yellowish fourplex home.

"Okay, make yourself at home. I gotta piss bad," Shiesty said as he kicked off his shoes and staggered through the house.

Aryana walked through the house, admiring its tidiness and all of the expensive-looking things in it. The place was far from what she'd expected it to be when he told her he had his own place.

"This is a nice place you have. I'm impressed," she complimented.

"Yeah, thanks. I own it. My OG left it to me when she died," he lied. His mother was alive and well, doing time for killing her boyfriend in a cocaine-fueled fight over the last rock.

"Sorry to hear that."

"Thanks, but my bad for bringing it up. I just be missin' her so much . . ."

Aryana cut the rest of the lie off by kissing him. Shiesty was too drunk to think past getting between her legs, so he accepted her tongue in his mouth. Their tongues did a slow dance while he pushed up the back of her skirt and palmed her bare booty that he found beneath it. Without breaking for long, she removed his shirt. Aryana's eyes lit up when she saw how chiseled his body was. Shiesty had the build of a Greek god, and just the sight of it had her juices flowing. Right then, she made up her mind to allow him to have his way with her.

Even in his drunken haze, Shiesty didn't miss the fresh glimmer of lust in her eyes. Tightening his grip on her soft behind, he easily scooped her up in his hands, and she instantly wrapped her legs around his waist and her lips on his neck. Shiesty carried her into his bedroom and aggressively tossed her down onto his unmade bed and began snatching off the little clothing she had on. Seeing her freshly waxed mound smiling invitingly back at him, Shiesty slithered headfirst between her knees.

Ogling him, Aryana wrapped her hands around her knees, pulling them wide to ensure Shiesty's flickering tongue landed where she needed to feel it. Her eyes rolled when he dragged his tongue through her slit, pausing to suck her clit for a moment or two before repeating.

"Oh, shit, yes!" she moaned, unconsciously slapping him on the top of his head.

Her blow didn't cause him to miss a beat. Shiesty continued dragging his tongue up and down, circling her throbbing clit with an intensity she didn't expect from her mark. As soon as he felt her legs quiver, he pulled back, then dragged his cum-soaked tongue up her warm torso until his lips reached her tiny breasts, and his hard tip parted her creaming knoll. Locked between her long legs in a sloppy missionary position, the two sucked and licked on one another's neck and face like animals. Shiesty rammed his thickness deep inside her sloppy box, and she growled with pleasure.

"Harder, harder—get this pussy. Get it!" she said, sucking on his bottom lip as he slammed in and out of her wetness.

The way she clawed his back told him he was giving it to her the way she needed him to. He roughly flipped her over onto her stomach, slid right into her from the back, and fucked her as fast and as hard as he could. He could feel sweat gathering on his neck and back as he continued to fuck her the way she kept telling him to.

"Bitch, you like this dick, don't you?" he inquired, simultaneously smacking her phat booty hard after each word.

"I'm cumming again!" she screamed.

Hearing that made him speed up his strokes until he couldn't take it anymore and erupted on her cum-soaked butt cheeks. Spent, he rolled off and fell right asleep beside her.

Chapter 11

Jaheim was awakened by Sentrice grinding her butt up against his length. Without her saying a word, she told him exactly what she wanted. So he pushed her away, flipped her over, and pulled her over him, sliding easily into her fiery depths. Sentrice didn't mind putting in the work to get what she craved in the early hour. She rode him hard and fast, not holding back her lust or her juices. Afterwards, they lay in one another's sweat-covered arms, breathing heavily from the hot morning session of pleasure and release they'd given each other.

"Can I use your shower?"

"Sure, but are you getting ready to leave?" she inquired, hating the way she sounded immediately after questioning him.

"As much as I don't want to go, I gotta . . ."

"No, don't. You don't have to explain. I understand," Sentrice softly kissed him, then nodded. "You can use the bathroom in the hallway," she said, watching him slide out of the bed, still looking as good as he did through her drunken gaze the night before.

She continued to watch her mind-blowing one-night stand awkwardly scurry around her place nude, collecting his clothing before disappearing behind the guest bathroom door. Sentrice was about to get up herself when she received a text message from her brother reminding her that they had a job scheduled for that afternoon and to meet him at the clubhouse. A short time later, she was walking Jaheim to the door, accepting his kiss and promise to call her before he briskly walked to his car with his eyes glued to his phone.

Sentrice thought about not going on the job and just crawling back in bed, but she couldn't leave her brother's life in the hands of the others. So, she put on coffee, then went into the master bathroom and got herself together.

Three hours later, she sat in the back of DB's truck, watching her brother do what he always did before a job. Bomani slipped on a pair of black latex gloves, then checked the magazine in his gun, already knowing that it was fully loaded, and then slammed it into the base of his M-4. He replaced his simple black mask with a strategically chosen designer one. She wondered who helped him pick out his mask since it wasn't her. For this lick, he'd chosen the face of Pennywise, the clown from the movie *IT*.

Okay, my plug call and hang up, I know what that mean / Give him 'bout twenty minutes / We'll rendezvous and he'll hit me off with them things / I play wholesale, I'm not breaking down, I got no use for no beam / But we wide open, my spot rollin' like a yo-yo with no string . . .

Sentrice watched the three of them bob their heads to their favorite song by Starlito and Don Trip. The boss turned in the seat so he was facing his collaborators seated in the Durango with him, pleased to see everyone dressed to move.

"*Sis, keep in mind that we're going in here to break these fools,*" Sentrice said, mimicking her big brother's predictable speech.

"Yeah, yeah, bro, I know. I'ma be a good girl."

"You better be," he retorted.

"I don't wanna hear it when you need me. And just so you know, tonight we're voting on a new song. It's about time, don't you think?" Sentrice smiled, stuck her tongue out at him, then pulled up her new mask with the slogan *Say Her Name* written in bright gold letters over her face.

Sentrice was still beaming from the wonderful time she'd had with Jaheim. She zoned out thinking—wondering if she messed up things by allowing him to take her down too fast. She wondered if he would call her like he said he would and if he did, would it only be for sex because he thought she was a hoe.

"Shiesty, you ready, homie?" Bomani asked.

"You know I'm always ready, Bobo," he answered from behind his mask.

"DB, you know the drill. Keep this muthafucka hot."

"I'll be here waiting and ready, as always," DB responded, then noticed Sentrice's goofy, spacey smile as she stared out the window. "Sen! Sen? Earth to, Sentrice!" he exclaimed, snapping her out of her thoughts.

"Whaaaaat?" she answered, showing her annoyance with his interruption.

"You good? You with us, or is you still on whoever tapped that last night?" DB asked, a knowing grin plastered on his face.

"Man, don't get her started," Bomani said, then saw the opening he was waiting on. "Y'all ready? 'Cuz it's go time," he announced, switching off the safety on his weapon.

DB gave Bomani a thumbs up, pressed repeat on the song, and laughed when Sentrice flipped him a double middle-finger salute before she followed the others out of the truck. As always, DB sat in the getaway car, keeping watch while wishing he could be inside on the action.

Chapter 12

Bomani had been fantasizing and preparing for the day he no longer had to rob and steal to keep a roof over his head and put food on the table. He loved the rush of running up in the places they'd robbed almost as much as he loved getting the drugs and money they took from them. But Bomani loved his sister more than all of it, and pulling out of life's fast lane was the best way for him to show his love to her.

Now, back in the safety of their clubhouse after another successful mission, Bomani decided to use the time to let Sentrice and everyone else know his plans for the future.

"Alright, everybody!" he began. "Y'all know the rules—they're the same as always. Don't be out there ballin' like it ain't no tomorrow," Bomani said, watching Shiesty ease off into the kitchen. "Now it's more important than ever that we stay low-key, especially since we're about to hit the cartel directly," he said, placing a duffle bag of cash on the table and issuing out everyone's cuts of the money inside.

"Bump all that! It's party like it's 2019!" Shiesty exclaimed, walking from the kitchen with large bottles of *Armand de Brignac*—also known as Ace of Spades—champagne in each hand.

Shiesty popped open one of the bottles and began filling red plastic cups with the expensive champagne. When Bomani placed Shiesty's share of the money down in front of him, he gulped down his cup, then started doing his celebratory Floss dance.

"Fool, calm down!" Bomani said, laughing and shaking his head at his friend's clownishness.

"Don't hate!" Shiesty retorted, speeding up the dance and laughing at himself. "I'd like to make a toast," he announced, getting everyone's attention.

"Chill yo ass out! I got this," Bomani said to Shiesty.

"Checked 'im!" Sentrice exclaimed, teasing Shiesty.

"Whatever, Sen. How 'bout you check this?" he shot back, giving her the middle finger.

The back-and-forth between Shiesty and Sentrice was normal. Even though they acted like they hated one another, when the time came, they always had each other's back.

"Both of y'all chill, damn!" Bomani snapped, regaining control of the room. "Now, the real reason for celebration isn't this bread in front of us. It's that it was done without leaving a bloodbath behind. In and out smooth, like the old days. Cheers to Sen for a job well done. I thought that loud crying-ass bitch was a goner when she wouldn't shut up when you told her," Bomani said honestly, as they raised their cups to her, then took a sip.

"You've been acting strange today," Shiesty said, playfully sniffing the air near Sentrice, then asked, "Who you been giving that lil funky monkey to?"

"Funky is them two-dollar hoes you be fuckin' with. Get it right. It's never funky this way!" she shot back at him. "And who I have in my bed is none of nobody's business but my own!"

"Shiesty, why? Why would you start back fuckin' with her? You know once she gets started on you . . ." DB asked, shaking his head.

"Anywaaaays! If you let me finish—and if it *is* a knucklehead nigga sniffing around, I'ma deal with it," Bomani said, giving his sister a threatening stare.

Sentrice was about to say something snappy when suddenly her cellphone began vibrating, distracting her train of thought. She fished the phone out of her back pocket, right away seeing that she'd received a text from an unknown number.

"Whatever!" she said to her brother's comment.

"Hey y'all, two weeks from tomorrow we're going to be doing our last lick. Once we hit the cartel's transport, we're done. I'm out. I'm trading in my gun for cold drinks and sunshine somewhere in Georgia."

"What you mean by 'we're done'?" Sentrice inquired, simultaneously opening the text message from the unknown number.

"I mean no more hittin' licks. We're 100% done after we bust this last move."

"Bo, are you serious?" Shiesty asked, no longer laughing.

"I'm serious—dead-ass serious," Bomani answered. "If y'all been following the plan we made from the beginning, then we all should have enough money put up to retire on. If not, then after we hit this last lick, you'll have enough to get on something new. Either way, I'm out. But I need to thank all y'all because without each of you having my back and doing your part, none of this would have been possible," Bomani said, raising his cup in a second toast. But no one joined him. "Really? Y'all gonna leave me hangin'? Look, it's time. We can't keep doing this shit forever. I've been planning this last lick as our endgame long before I ever said shit to y'all about it. I've already scoped out the cartel driver's routes and our getaway routes. When they come to do the cash pick-ups, there's always three of them: a money man, a bodyguard, and a lookout-slash-driver. This is gonna be a piece of cake," he explained.

"The only difference in this lick from the others is we gonna have to use two cars. Half of the money will go in one car and the other half in the other. So . . . DB, buddy, I'ma need you to break out your old bag of tricks and get us a couple of whips that's nice and fast. I'll be in the car with you."

"Dawg, man, bro! Why I gotta ride with Ms. Crabby Patty?" Shiesty whined.

"I put y'all together because I know if things get hot what she gon' do, and I know with you behind the wheel, y'all will get away safe."

"When is the latest that I need to have the cars by?" DB asked, exhaling a cloud of weed smoke as he helped himself to another glass of champagne.

"It don't matter as long as you got 'em before the day of," Bomani answered.

"Bro, it sounds like you got everything all decided for us," Sentrice said without looking up from her phone as she read and replied to the message that read:

"Hey, Gorgeous, this is Jaheim. I'm sitting here wondering if you're not too busy, would you allow me to take you out to eat since I had to rush out this morning . . ."

Sentrice replied: *"Sure, I'm just finishing up at work, but I have a nail appointment in 45 minutes. I'll text you afterwards, or do you have a time set already?"*

"No, no time. I'll be waiting."

After making the date, Sentrice put her phone back in her pocket with a big smile on her face.

"Who that got you smiling all of a sudden?" Bomani inquired, curious because she hadn't mentioned to him that she was seeing anyone.

"I called it!" Shiesty exclaimed. "Someone's got a boyfriend! Someone's got a boyfriend!" he sang, once again doing the Floss dance.

"Grow up!" she barked, rolling her eyes. "Who my friend is, is my business until I'm ready for y'all to meet him. Now, like I was saying—bro, you've decided for us already, so there's nothing more to say. Hold on to my money for me 'cuz I have a nail appointment, then I gotta get ready for my date."

Bomani walked Sentrice out to her car so they were out of earshot of the others. That's when he told her he was planning on moving out of Milwaukee for good.

"Sis, I'm thinking of moving down to Georgia, not just going to visit," he confessed while holding her car door open for her.

"When?"

"After we bust this move. I think it'll be good for us."

"Bro, this is . . . sudden. Let's talk about it later, 'cuz I gotta go," Sentrice said, pulling her door shut and swiftly driving off.

Chapter 13

Newly partnered detectives Tonya Lont and Dave Hermon were just finishing up collecting what little evidence they could find from the latest robbery. Everything about the robbery fit the robbery crew they were tracking, except no one was killed in this one. Though it was a good thing, the sudden change in motive altered Lont's entire working profile.

"Tonya, we gotta go now! A patrolman thinks he may have one of our robbery suspects pulled over a few blocks from here," Detective Hermon yelled from the car window.

Lont immediately slid into the passenger's seat, and Hermon sped off with full lights and sirens. Within seconds, they were parked beside the lone officer's patrol car.

"So, what do we have here? What makes you believe that's one of our guys?" Lont asked the patrolman.

"I've been following your robbery-homicide case from the start because I'm hoping to make detective soon," he confessed, then quickly ran down a list of suspicions that the driver of the SUV fit into.

"Good enough for me. Let's bring him in for the DUI and let him sleep it off before questioning," Lont said.

"Okay, I'll go get him," the officer said, then broke away from the two detectives.

The officer noticed the suspect fidgeting around inside the SUV, so he drew his weapon and slowed his approach.

"Sir, place your left hand on the wheel and open the door from the outside with the other. Then slowly exit the truck with your hands where I can see them!"

The detectives could hear the officer giving the suspect orders but couldn't make out his responses. Then, all of a sudden, the suspect shot the officer. He sprang from the vehicle, immediately sending shots at the detectives. Lont and Hermon dived out of the way just as the bullets whizzed past them, destroying the windshield of the police car. Lont rolled and jumped to her feet, squeezing her trigger as the suspect dropped back into the SUV and sped off.

"Officer down! Repeat, officer down! Requesting immediate backup. Two plainclothes detectives are on the scene!" Hermon screamed into his radio, then joined his partner in attempting to stop the fleeing vehicle.

Lont's shots took out the rear window, while Hermon's shot out the rear tire, causing the SUV to spin out of control, jump the curb, and come to a crashing stop only after destroying the front porch of a vacant house.

"Toss out your weapon and step out of the vehicle with your hands up where I can see them!" Hermon bellowed, his gun trained on the back of the suspect's head.

Both detectives watched as the suspect got out of the wreckage and collapsed face-down on the lawn, unconscious.

Chapter 14

Jaheim ogled Sentrice as she exited her home. She was dressed in a violet vest and a matching Kenneth Cole chiffon dress. Her hair was styled the same way it was when they met the night before and looked just as good. She wore a pair of sparkling, dancing diamond hoop earrings dangling from her lobes and a smile that made him miss her lips on his.

Sentrice's smile widened when her eyes fell on him sitting in his gleaming Maserati Ghibli with his cellphone in hand. She immediately sashayed over and slid into the passenger seat. That's when Jaheim noticed she was wearing open-toe Aldo sandals, showing off her fresh French tip pedicure.

"Don't hang up because of me," she said, no longer smiling.

"I wasn't on the phone with anybody. I was about to text you," he explained and held his phone up so she could see her number on the screen.

"In that case, it's nice to see you again," she said, reigniting her smile.

"You say that like you wasn't sure you would," he commented as he pulled out into traffic. "So how was your day?"

"Nerve-wrecking," she let out an audible sigh and said. "Can we change the subject? Cuz I honestly don't wanna talk about it."

"That's fine, I was just making small talk."

"Sooo, where are you taking me?"

"I'm taking you to a nice little place that specializes in different types of fancy global cuisines."

"Sounds interesting, especially the way you described it. Do you get a discount or something for everyone you get to come there?" she giggled, teasing him.

"Ha-ha!" he said, flashing his dimpled smile while simultaneously pressing play on the car radio.

The song *Spark* by Trey Songz, featuring Jacquees, filled the air, creating a nice mellow mood to ride to. By the end of the song, they were pulling into a parking slot at the restaurant. Jaheim shut off the engine and stepped out. Sentrice noticed that he was casually dressed in a plain, crisp white button-up shirt and indigo soft leather pants, all by Polo Ralph Lauren, paired with white Nike Air Force Ones.

Showing her that chivalry isn't dead, Jaheim briskly walked around to the passenger's side and opened the door for his lovely date. Sentrice stepped out into the warm air, intertwined her arm in his, and the two entered the restaurant just like that.

Due to the strict COVID-19 restrictions, the place wasn't crowded, which made the atmosphere inside the establishment a lot more private and romantic. A cheerful young hostess greeted them at the door, then led the lovely couple to their reserved table.

"Someone will be here shortly to take your orders," she informed them, handing each an entrée menu and only one wine menu before returning to her post.

"So, what do you think? Is this nice enough for you?" Jaheim inquired, speaking over the soft whine of classical music playing through the restaurant's surround sound system.

"So far, so good. Ask me again after we get our food."

As promised, a waiter appeared to take their orders. Since Sentrice couldn't decide, Jaheim ordered Potato Chaat and Aloo Tikki for both of them, along with a nice white wine.

When his eyes returned to Sentrice, she seemed to be beaming.

"What?"

"Nothing. I just never had my man order for me before. It's nice," she confessed.

"Oh, so I'm your man now?" he asked without breaking their eye contact.

"I didn't mean it like that, but would that be a bad thing if I did?"

"I'll let you know after you taste what I ordered for us," he answered as the waiter returned, refilled their glasses with wine, and vanished again to retrieve their food.

"I can't wait," Sentrice said seductively, licking her lips before taking a sip of her wine.

"As much as I'm enjoying ogling you right now, the reason for this date is for us to get to know each other. So tell me—what's on your mind right now?"

"Honestly, I was just thinking how rare it is these days to come across a man who takes time to treat a woman the way you're treating me right now. Especially after our little after-party last night."

"Don't forget our good morning party. I know I won't," he chuckled and smiled.

"Believe it or not, this isn't my usual behavior. I don't just bring guys into my home or lay down with them on day one."

"That's good to know. But I kinda figured as much. That's why I'm here with you now. This COVID-19 bullshit has changed us all in one way or another—it's just everyday stress. So don't feel no kinda way about letting your hair down. I feel like the spark that connected us when we met was more than just us hooking up for the night. Even now, I want to know more, and I'm not in a rush to get away from you," he admitted just as his phone rang. "Give me a second, this my cousin in prison."

Sentrice sipped on her glass of sweet white wine and admired Jaheim's handsomeness while he talked on the phone. Then out of nowhere, her brother's admission about thinking about moving to Georgia came to mind. Sentrice knew that more than likely, Bomani would try to persuade her to move down south with him. And now that she'd met someone she likes, she wasn't ready to go anywhere.

"What are you over there thinking about?" Jaheim asked, snapping her out of her thoughts.

"My brother," she answered just as the waiter reappeared with their food. "Umm, this smells good."

"Do you wanna talk about it, or is it a private family issue?" he asked, then thanked the waiter to send him away.

"No, it's nothing like that. He told me that he's moving to Georgia." She paused to take a bite of her food. "Mmm, this is really good," she praised, then immediately ate more and washed it down with wine.

"I'm glad you like it cuz it's one of my favorites," he confessed, then asked, "Do you have family in Georgia?"

"No, it's just the two of us. My parents are deceased, and I don't know if we have anybody down there. And if we do, I wouldn't call them family."

"I'm sorry," he said sincerely.

"My brother and I are really close, and I think he's expecting me to move there with him."

"You don't wanna go, do you?"

"Honestly? Honestly, no," Sentrice said, looking Jaheim in his eyes. "I think I really wanna explore this I'm feeling for you. It's been a long time since I felt this way about anyone."

Her words caught him off guard. Truthfully, he felt the same way but didn't want to scare Sentrice away by saying it aloud.

"It's what I want," he told her, then kissed her hand.

"I want y'all to meet, and I want you there when I tell him I'm not moving."

"Okay, I don't have a problem meeting your brother or being your support."

Sentrice's smile returned to her pretty full lips. She wondered if Bomani would approve of Jaheim, because he never approved of any of the others she'd allowed to meet him.

"Can we get this to go? Suddenly, I'm really hungry for something else." She squeezed his hand as she ran her leg up and down his leg beneath the table.

"Yeah, we can get outta here. I'm looking at what I got a taste for," he retorted in a sexually charged tone. Jaheim called the waiter over and asked for the check, the bottle of wine, and two to-go bags.

Chapter 15

Bomani reentered the house after walking his sister to her car. DB was right there waiting for him with a cup of champagne.

"What's in Georgia?" DB asked, handing him the drink.

"Man, it's a new start with new people and no ghosts. I'm about tired of just existing. It's time to live, don't you think?" Bomani responded, accepting the cup and taking a sip. "Milwaukee has been good to us, but it's also been hard on Sen. You see it. She needs to go somewhere where she can just kick her feet up and mentally heal from everything. We both do."

"So you just gonna move and leave us up here like . . . like . . ." DB's frustration was clear in his voice.

"Leave y'all up here like what? We've all hit the same licks and walked away with the same bread. So if y'all did right with the cash, then you can do whatever," Bomani said, looking at his friend with confusion.

"We're a family, and if you leave, you'll be breaking up the family."

"You right, we are family. Like I just said, I'm not stopping you from doing nothing. Y'all more than welcome to come with us," he offered.

After finishing about one of the two bottles of champagne and a quarter of a bottle of Comoveda Tequila, DB was good and in his feelings. He decided to just call it a night. He got up, exited the house, and got in his truck.

"Say, y'all, I'm gone!" he yelled over his shoulder on his way out.

The intoxicated driver cruised through the streets at a normal speed, but DB's SUV was swerving a little—not enough to concern him, though. He didn't feel like he couldn't make it home. As he zigzagged through the streets, DB began thinking about his own future. DB had never been outside of Wisconsin for anything other than a robbery with the team.

"I see now that that nigga never cared about nobody but his damn self and his bitch-ass sister!" he exclaimed aloud, slamming his hand against the steering wheel.

DB had always harbored romantic feelings for Bomani, who he suspected was bisexual. Bomani wasn't as open with his sex life as Shiesty, nor had he ever had an encounter with DB or given him a reason to believe he was into him. DB felt like, in Bomani's eyes, he was nothing more than a getaway driver. He was constantly asking Bomani to allow him to prove his worth on a job, but he was always told that he needed him to drive. That angered him and made him jealous of Sentrice.

Sentrice was a good driver, but Bomani showed her favoritism, even after she'd made things hot for them by always shooting or killing somebody when they did a job.

"Fuck Bo, and fuck Sen!" he shouted into the night air, now slightly speeding over the posted limit.

Suddenly, his cellphone began playing the ringtone he'd set for Bomani, startling him. Rushing to retrieve the phone from his hip to catch the call caused him to take his eyes off the road for a second too long. The truck swerved, almost sideswiping a row of parked cars.

Just as quickly as DB jerked the steering wheel away to prevent the collision, a police car's flashing lights went on behind him.

"Fuck!" he exclaimed. Then he remembered the Taco Bell bag filled with money and his gun lying on the passenger seat beside him. "Fuck! Fuck! Fuck! I can't go to jail!" he cursed, grabbing the gun and placing it on his lap as he pulled over. Following the statewide mask mandate, he immediately put on his mask.

Nervously, DB sat up in his seat and watched as the lone officer exited the cruiser and cautiously approached.

"Is everything alright in here?" the officer inquired once he was standing at DB's window.

"Yeah . . . yeah, sir, everything's fine," DB answered with a slight slur that the officer didn't miss.

"License and insurance, please?" The officer watched as DB retrieved his wallet and handed over both cards.

"I noticed you ran off the road back there," the officer told him. "Have you been drinking tonight?"

"I had a glass of champagne for my boss's retirement, but I'm not drunk, sir—just tired. I dropped my phone, that's why that happened back there, sir," DB explained with a nervous grin.

"I see. Sit tight—I'll be right back."

The officer briskly marched back to the cruiser and got in. Watching the officer through the rearview mirror, thoughts of paranoia began to take over DB's intoxicated mind. He didn't like the way the officer had suddenly walked away and wondered if he'd seen the gun sitting between his legs when he moved to give him the cards. Then, a second police car pulled up to the scene. DB noticed that it was an unmarked detective car, which made him watch them more closely through the mirror.

A short time later, the officer broke away from the two detectives and approached DB more cautiously than before.

"Sir, place your left hand on the wheel and open the door with your right from the outside. Then slowly exit the car with your hands where I can see them."

"Is there a problem, officer?" DB glanced at the detectives through the rearview mirror.

"Step out of the vehicle now, please!" the officer commanded, his gun in hand at his side.

"What's this about?" DB questioned, making up his mind that he wasn't going easy. He clutched his Glock 27, pushed open the door, then quickly raised his gun and shot the officer several times in the chest. He then stepped out, immediately sending shots at the detectives standing behind the car. They dived out of the way just as the bullets whizzed past them, destroying the windshield of the police car.

DB dropped back into the truck, threw it into drive, and stomped the accelerator. The powerful Hemi engine in the Durango made the tires scream as it jetted off. DB had to duck when the detectives started returning fire. He almost crashed when a bullet shattered the back window and slammed into the dashboard.

One of the detectives' shots hit the left rear tire of the speeding SUV. DB spun out of control, jumped the curb, and crashed into the front porch of a vacant house. The impact from the collision caused DB's head to slam into the window, opening a deep three-inch gash across his forehead when he turned away from the airbag.

Dazed and bloody, DB managed to open his door and get out, only to collapse on the lawn before he could make a run for it. The next time his eyes opened, he was surrounded by cops with their guns trained on him, shouting for him to toss his gun and stay down. He passed out again, involuntarily surrendering.

Chapter 16

The two hot aficionados barely made it all the way through the front door of Sentrice's home before their mouths and hands were all over each other. Like newlyweds, Jaheim and Sentrice tore off one another's clothing as they pushed farther inside. When Jaheim got her out of her dress, he took a breather to admire her, then dropped to his knees and began kissing and sucking Sentrice's thick, thick thighs, teasingly moving from one to the other, before savagely ripping at her thong with his teeth.

Sentrice pushed her blossom to his face, and his tongue went right where she needed it to stroke. Sentrice freed her hair, letting it fall wildly over her shoulders. She couldn't resist loudly moaning as the excited tiny figure eights of her lover's tongue skated around her clit, giving her the sweet pleasure she craved.

"Oh shit! You, you—you!" Sentrice mumbled as she dropped her leg over his strong shoulder. "Ooooh gawd! Mmm! I can't take it! I can't . . . I'm a cumming!" she shouted, bouncing and pounding her hips with clenched fists.

Jaheim abruptly stopped, stood up, and scooped her off her feet. He carried her over to the dining room table. There, Sentrice broke free of his hold, dropped down, and took his tip in her mouth. She swirled her tongue around it a few times, then gobbled as much of his hard, throbbing pole into her warm, wet mouth as she could.

She hummed when she felt his fingers sliding through her hair. She jagged him with a tight fist between servings of her oral delight.

He allowed her to have her way right up until he felt his toes begin to curl. That's when he pulled Sentrice to her feet, picked her up, and carried her into the bedroom. There, he gently placed her on the edge of the bed and slowly entered her as they simultaneously kissed and nibbled on one another's lips, neck, and lips some more.

"Harder, Jaheim!" she purred in his ear. "Fuck me harder, baby! It's yours, baby!"

Sentrice spread her legs wider, giving him room to thrust even harder. She bit her bottom lip and watched his hardness disappear in and out of her, pounding her wetness fast, then slow, hard, then soft.

"Jah! Jah! Oh my God, Jaheim!" Sentrice bellowed as her legs trembled, sending shockwaves up her entire body.

"Oh, shit!" Jaheim ululated out of breath, followed by a growl as he shot his powerful eruption inside her sopping blossom.

Afterwards, lying in each other's arms, sticky with sex and sweat, Sentrice was the first to break the silence.

"It's crazy when a bad day can bring me a man like the one I've been looking for all of my life."

"Yeah, that is. But why are you so sure that I'm that nigga when we ain't known each other but a hot second? And what happens when you meet someone better tomorrow?" he challenged her.

"That's not happening. Especially with the way you just put it on me. I'm not saying you got me blinded for only you, but . . ." She giggled.

"So, in the end, you just said I got you blinded?" he chuckled.

"Don't laugh!" she said, hitting him with a pillow and rolling out of bed to avoid retaliation.

He was getting ready to respond when he heard LaQuess's ringtone.

"You lucky. I have to get that," he said as he got up and jogged into the other room to catch the call.

"Hey, Cuzo, whud up?" he answered.

"Jah, I put the word out on that lick you told me about, and my girl Ayrana thinks she's fuckin' with one of them. She said he been flaunting phat-ass bankrolls, splurging since she met him. You need to get over here right now and talk to her about him."

"Say no mo, I'll be there in a few."

"Cuz, she's supposed to go meet up with the nigga in a lil bit, so don't take all day."

"Tell her to sit tight. I'm walking outta the door right now."

Jaheim ended the call as he walked back into the bedroom where Sentrice waited.

"Ma, I'm sorry, but something just came up that I gotta go handle right quick."

"Awww!" she groaned, then asked, "Are you coming back afterwards? Because I was really looking forward to waking up in your arms tomorrow."

"I don't know how late it'll be by the time I get done, but if you don't mind the time, then yeah, I'll be back."

Sentrice got up, walked over to the dresser, retrieved the spare key from her jewelry box, and handed it to him.

"I don't care how late it is, just come back," she said, then kissed him and pushed him toward the bathroom. "You better go get me off you before you go rushing outta here."

Jaheim looked down at the key in his hand and smiled before disappearing into the bathroom.

Chapter 17

Sitting across the street from LaQuess's place, Jaheim felt a little spike of adrenaline when he received the text from his cousin informing him that Ayrana was walking outside to meet the guy they believed was one of the jack boys Chief Ken had asked him to eliminate.

Jaheim couldn't make a move without Ayrana because there were two vehicles with occupants waiting for someone parked out front of the apartment building. One was a Care Bear-themed 1970 Chevy Nova with two guys inside it, and the other was a BMW with one person in it, who'd been talking on the phone since he'd pulled up and parked. Knowing it was a crew of at least five people he was looking for, it would've been reckless to make a move on a wild assumption. So he waited until the car was about halfway down the block before pulling off and following behind them. Knowing from the bodies the crew had been leaving behind, Jaheim called a couple of his guys for assistance.

Inside, Shiesty went to work trying to impress Ayrana by taking her into his bedroom and pulling out the bag of cash from his robbery earlier.

"Yeah, you see it! You see it—whatever you want, I got it. As soon as my nigga bitch get here, we going to party it up in this bitch!" he said, pulling her over to him.

"Can I use your bathroom real quick?" she asked.

"You remember where it's at," he replied, tapping her on the butt before she walked away.

Shiesty went into the kitchen to get drinking glasses for them. He was filling a bowl with ice when he heard the doorbell over the music. He yelled out to his guy to answer the door, assuming it was the other girl they were expecting. Instead of giggling, Shiesty heard angry male voices coming from the other room. He stopped what he was doing in the kitchen to go see what the fuss was about. Caught by surprise, Shiesty was knocked in the temple with a gun and slammed onto the floor by a man with a large black mask covering most of his face.

"I told you I don't know what or who you're talkin' 'bout, and I don't have shit here! Now get out of my crib!" Shiesty lied to the masked men who were holding guns menacingly on him and his friend.

In the bathroom, exchanging texts with LaQuess about what was going on, Ayrana also heard the doorbell followed by the shouting. She cracked the bathroom door, being nosey. The last thing she wanted was for Shiesty to know she had anything to do with whatever was going on between him and LaQuess's fine-ass cousin. But she couldn't help herself from listening in.

"Stop lying, bitch-ass nigga! Tell me where the rest of yo' guys at before I spill your thoughts all over the fuckin' place!" Jaheim barked, holding his gun on Shiesty.

Ayrana figured she'd go steal herself a few stacks of cash from the bag of money so she wouldn't be leaving empty-handed when it was over. She took a few steadying breaths, then crept out of the bathroom.

"Fuck you! I can't tell you what I don't know, and if I did tell you, why would you let me live to tell anyone that you're coming for 'em? So until you get what you're lookin' for, you're not going to shoot me. So fuck you!" Shiesty said, a sure defiance in his tone as he stood up.

Jaheim menacingly chuckled, shaking his head before suddenly backhanding Shiesty with the gun. That's when

Shiesty's friend tried to make a move, taking a wild swing at one of the men with Jaheim.

"Punk, what? You think you're tough? Fuck you!" Jaheim's guy exclaimed, squeezing his trigger twice. The shots hit Shiesty's friend once in the throat and once in his upper chest.

In the hall outside of the bathroom, Ayrana jumped at the loud booms and covered her mouth in terror, muffling her own scream. With her heart now racing, she instantly abandoned her get-rich scheme and hid in the bathtub to save herself.

This was the first time Shiesty had been on the other side of a situation like the ones he'd put so many others in. He had no reason to think things wouldn't go the way they would if he and his team were the ones with the guns.

"Whoa, whoa! Hold up, my nigga!" Shiesty cried out, putting his hands up in surrender. "I got, like, a bunch of money in the back on the bed. Y'all can have it all, and I won't say shit," he bargained, thinking of his chances of survival. "Hey, hey, you don't know what you're getting yourself in . . ."

Suddenly, Shiesty moved quickly counterclockwise and brought his arm down, trying to knock the gun out of Jaheim's hand. Jaheim automatically squeezed the trigger, accidentally hitting his partner in the shoulder with the first shot and putting the other shots in the floor and wall. Shiesty shoved him, spun, and ran for his life.

"Hey, stop!" Jaheim yelled, taking aim at the fleeing man's back. "Don't move!"

Shiesty didn't stop. Everything in him at that moment told him if he stopped, they were going to kill him. So he ran toward the back of the house. Angry shots whizzed by him, hitting everything around him. Without slowing, he burst through the back door. Outside, he sprinted across the backyard and through to the neighboring yards. Shiesty's only thought was getting as far away as possible, fast. He flattened himself against the side of a house, trying to catch his breath. His heart was pounding hard as he listened and prayed he wasn't followed.

He peeked behind him first, and after seeing the coast was clear, he peeked around the front of the house and saw two cars racing away in opposite directions. He was sure they were the men from his house, going to try and catch him on the next block someplace. Whatever they were doing, he wasn't going back in the house to be certain. He sprinted to his car and stormed off, not giving Ayrana's wellbeing a moment of thought.

Chapter 18

It was around 10 a.m. when Detective Lont clocked into work at the precinct and instructed the desk sergeant to have the robbery suspect, who was fresh from the hospital, placed in the interrogation room. With that done, Lont headed to the break room and poured two coffees—one black for her suspect and the other with sugar and creamer for herself.

The detective ambled down the corridor to the interrogation room, collecting her thoughts from the morning meeting before she interviewed her hungover and possibly concussed robbery suspect. She hoped that after he'd spent the night sleeping his drunk off, he would be willing to tell her something she could use to close the case on the violent robberies.

Lont paused when she reached the door to briefly converse with her partner, who proudly stood there wearing a Blue Lives Matter mask and dressed in a white, two-tone blue-striped polo shirt and tan slacks with scuffed black soft-bottom shoes. He planned to be watching her closely from the observation room and recording her interview of the suspect.

"Is one of those for me?" Hermon inquired, pointing toward the two cups in her hands.

"No, I'm sorry. I would've brought you one had I known you were going to be here, but I need this here for Mr. Sunshine in there."

"Are you sure you want to go in there alone?"

"Yeah, I'm sure," Lont answered, and Hermon nodded before disappearing into the observation room next door. Once Lont was alone again, she took a deep breath, then entered the room with a friendly smile on her face.

Right away, she noticed DB's bruised face from its collision with the airbag a few hours before. Her intuition told her that he wasn't a cold-blooded killer. DB wasn't acting like a murderous outlaw at all. Being honest, she thought he was a bit dainty, but she'd learned a long time ago not to judge a book by its cover.

"Good afternoon, Mr. Barnet, or do you prefer to be called DB?" she asked, placing the coffee in front of him and simultaneously taking a seat in the chair across the table from him.

"DB is fine." He looked at the steaming cup of coffee and asked, "Is this for me?"

"Yeah, after the night you had, I'm guessing you can use a nice strong cup," she admitted, raising her own cup to him. "I know after being shot at and taken on a short high-speed chase at the end of a long 12-hour shift, only to return to work after only a few hours of sleep, I sure in the hell need this cup." She paused to take in DB's demeanor. "Look here, I'm not going to bullshit you up in here. I know you don't want that, and I don't have time for it. You know you got yourself in a fucked-up situation."

"I-I-I don't remember doing any of what you said happened last night."

"You don't remember?" she repeated, surprised. "So that's what you want to do? Okay, let's just forget about the officer you shot, the chase, and the tens of thousands of dollars' worth of property damage you did last night. I don't care about that. Here's what I know about you, DB. I know that you are a member of the robbery crew that's been hitting all of the cartel's illegal cash spots, and you're on body cam shooting at us. You shot a cop!" She raised her voice, shaking her head. "Believe it or not, I'm here to help you out of this mess, but I'm going to need you to help me."

"Help you how?" he chuckled. "You just said I shot a cop on camera."

"Yeah, but you were drunk, and the bullet hit him in the vest. I just may be able to sweet-talk him into dropping the charge," she smiled, giving him a little wink with it.

"Okay, but I know all of the shit you say I did got me all over the news by now."

"It is all over the news, but not you. No one knows at this time about your arrest," she told him. "I made sure it was kept hushed just for this conversation."

"Okay, I'm listening," he said, raising his powder-blue hospital-issued mask slightly and taking a sip of his coffee.

"Good. So here are your options. One, you can tell me who your buddies are that helped you rob all those places and where to find them in exchange for the charges of drunk driving, fleeing, and criminal damage to property. Or, you can continue to play that weak amnesia card and end up spending the rest of your life in Waupun State Prison."

"If I cooperate, I won't be able to get charged with anything more than what you said?" DB asked, full of suspicion.

"That's right," Lont promised, nodding *yes* and sipping from her cup.

"I ain't stupid, Detective!"

"I never said you were."

"Then you know before I say another word, I'ma need you to give me that in writing."

"I'll be right back in a second." She then excused herself, leaving the room.

Lont walked next door into the observation room, where her captain and Hermon sat behind the two-way mirror watching and listening in on her interview of their suspect.

"Captain, I knew I'd find you in here. I need you to work your magic and get the DA to guarantee the deal so Mr. Man in there can give us his partners."

"I'm not guaranteeing that just for a list of fucking names!" the captain snapped. "He shot a cop, for Christ's sake! That piece of shit should sit in prison forever!"

"Captain, I'm not asking you to guarantee his total freedom. Just that our department will not charge him with the crimes that he committed when we got him. When he agrees, you can just hand him over to the Feds," she explained with a devious smile behind her plain black mask.

In the interrogation room, DB sat in deep thought. He was seriously considering the detective's proposal for him to give up the names and whereabouts of Bomani and the rest of the crew. DB whispered to himself, seriously trying to convince himself that if any of the others were in his position, they would flip on him in a heartbeat. His feelings were still hurt from Bomani's announcement about leaving him.

By the time the door opened for the detective's return, he had made up his mind that he had no other choice but to do what's needed to look out for himself.

"This is my captain. He has a slightly different deal to offer that I'm sure you would like," Lont explained to DB before she gave the floor to the captain to execute their plan.

"I'm not as forgiving as my detective when it comes to the shooting of one of my fellow officers. But I trust her judgment," the captain paused dramatically for a second, then explained the new terms of the deal offered for DB's cooperation. "Here's the deal. You're going to set up your partners so they will be caught in the act. In return for your cooperation, I'll promise you in writing that my department will not charge you with the three accounts of attempted homicide that you committed last night against my officers, nor will we charge you for the actions of your buddies. Let me make myself clear: If you in any way try to run or warn them, I'll personally nail your ass to the cross for it all!"

Lont could see the wheels turning in DB's head before he spoke, and she knew they had him.

"They got another hit planned in a few days, but I don't know the details of it. But it's not certain that it will happen—things change with him all of the time," DB admitted.

"Hold on, before you say another word, I need you to waive your right to have your attorney present for this discussion," Lont informed him. "You have the right to remain silent," she said, before reading him his rights.

Chapter 19

Hours passed without a word from Jaheim, and since Sentrice didn't want to come off as being the clingy, nagging type, she resisted her urge to call him. No matter how late it got, she resisted.

Around 2 a.m., she snapped awake, lying alone on the sofa where she'd fallen asleep waiting on Jaheim's return. An instant feeling of dread flooded over her when she checked her phone and saw that she'd missed calls and texts from him. He explained that one of his guys had been accidentally shot while they were together, and he had to rush him to the hospital.

Though disappointed that Jaheim wasn't there with his arms wrapped tightly around her, Sentrice was relieved that he was alright. Before him, the only person she'd ever worried about like that was her brother. Her brother was the only other man alive who could make her heart skip with joy. The first was her dad.

Her mind easily slipped into a fantasy of being a loving wife, the way she remembered her mother being to her father, when she came across a text from Jaheim promising to come straight to her after he picked up a change of clothing. Smiling from ear to ear, she responded to his text, apologizing for missing his calls and her tardy reply, then went back to sleep.

The next time her eyes opened, it was to the sound of a vehicle pulling into her driveway. Sentrice briskly skip-walked her way into the bathroom and peeked out the window. Her excitement diffused, changing to a bit of disappointment when she saw it was her brother and not her man. Instead of quickly getting herself together, she just threw on a short, peach-colored robe and went to answer the door for Bomani.

"Hey, big brother. What brings you to my house this early that you couldn't call me about?"

"Do you got company, or is you expecting somebody?" he inquired, noticing that she wasn't wearing the silk headscarf she always put on before bed.

"Not right now, but he should be here soon, so I hope the reason you're here for don't take long because I want you gone before he gets here," she said, walking away from the door.

"Why you ain't call me?" Bomani asked, entering and closing the door behind himself.

"I was busy," she exclaimed, rolling her eyes. "And call you about what?"

Bomani followed her into the kitchen, then made his way over to the refrigerator and poured himself a glass of orange juice.

"Whud up wit' what I said to you 'bout moving to Savannah, Georgia?" He downed almost half the glass of juice in one gulp.

"What you mean 'Whud up wit' it?" Sentrice asked with an attitude as she turned on the coffee maker.

"I mean, when are you gonna start packing? Or are you just gonna leave all this shit here and start from scratch?"

"My stuff is not shit, punk! And I'm not moving to no Georgia. Bo, everything I know is here."

"Fuck you mean you not going?" he demanded, slamming his glass of juice on the table, looking at his sister like she was out of her mind.

"I said I'm not going, and I meant what I said!" she retorted with her arms folded across her chest. She was tired of Bomani turning his dreams into her dreams and being afraid to say no to him. "I'm gonna stay here and build something of my own with my new boyfriend."

"New boyfriend! Who's this nigga that you tryna rush me outta here for anyway?" he snapped with his face frowned up. "How long you been fuckin' with 'im behind my back?"

"Long enough!"

"That's not an answer!" he shouted.

"It is, and it's the only one you're getting!"

Bomani fell silent, wondering how he had missed the signs that she was in a relationship. He was usually on point with things, especially when it came to his family.

"Sen, everything I had us doing and got planned for us is to get our money right so we'll be able to live good somewhere with no worries."

"I know." Sentrice softened her tone. "I know the plan, big brother. My *somewhere* is here. Georgia is for you. I'm not going."

"If you stay in the Mil, it's a chance that the police or somebody will figure out who we are sometime down the line," he said, trying to scare her into changing her mind.

"That's only if somebody talks, and if that happen, being down south ain't finna stop 'em from coming to get us," she stated.

"Sis, I know you think I don't wanna see you happy, but that's so not the truth. My main priority is to keep you happy and safe."

"Bomani, you've done all of that. You taught me everything I need to know to keep myself safe. I'm grown now and more than capable of taking care of myself."

Bomani huffed and dropped his head in thought. He loved Sentrice's stubbornness because it reminded him of their mom, but he also hated it.

"You know what? You're right. I'm not our daddy, and in the back of my mind, I know that you're capable of taking care of yourself. You know, I think it's just me being afraid of not having you to chase off all of the gold-diggin' hoes that I come across."

"Whoa! Who says I'm not going to be around for that? I'll jump on the first thing smoking to fuck a bitch up over you!"

The two of them laughed and hugged it out.

"On that thought, when are you going to bring yo guy around so I can beat him—I mean, meet him?" he chuckled.

"Leave mine alone," she said, playfully punching him in the chest.

"Ooo shit! You really like this one, don't you?"

"Yeah, I do. Jah is different than the others. He treats me right," Sentrice explained, beaming with pride.

"Maybe I'll stick around and meet him now when he gets here?" Bomani suggested.

"No, no, no! I got plans for him this morning. Plus, he's coming to relax after a hard night. Sooo, no—not now."

"Girl, I didn't need to hear that. Now you got a picture in my head that's burning my brain," he joked, shaking his head. "You know what? I'm gonna have a going-away party so you can bring him then."

"First, promise me that you gonna be nice to him if I bring him to the party?"

"I gotta put him to the test. I can't be leaving my baby sis in the care of a punk-ass nigga now, can I?" he responded with a chuckle as he headed to the door.

"Whatever! I know you're gonna like him—watch."

"Come pick up your money later before I go party it on one of my hoes."

"No, you won't, but I'll swing by when I come out the house," she promised with a wink and a smile. "Look, there go one of yo' funky hoes now calling you."

"That's where ya wrong. This Shiesty texting me to come by the spot ASAP," Bomani explained. "Love you, sis!"

"Love you more, big brother!" She hugged him, then playfully shoved him out of her house at the sound of Jaheim's ringtone playing on her phone.

Chapter 20

Immediately, the reality of what happened came rushing to Shiesty's mind. He sat there, looking around the clubhouse, wondering what he should do next. It was the only place he knew to go where no one outside of his team would know to look for him. High and exhausted, as soon as he settled down on the sofa and closed his eyes to think about what happened, he unknowingly dozed off.

When he woke up and looked at his watch, it read 11 a.m. He sat up and turned on the TV, hoping to catch some report about what was going on at his house. The weather report was on, so he went to the kitchen to get something to drink.

With a cold grape soda in hand, Shiesty trudged back to the TV just in time to catch a recap of the breaking news report. The reporter's words paralyzed him in mid-swallow. The reporter said that Shiesty was a person of interest in connection with the shooting death of a 22-year-old unknown female found dead in the bathroom of his home. She went on to say that witnesses placed Shiesty at the scene, as well as several other unknown males, at the time of the shooting. The reporter ended by informing viewers that they could find more information about the report on the news app.

Shiesty instantly went in search of his cellphone. When he found that it wasn't in his back pocket, where it usually was, he located it lying beside the sofa next to his car keys.

As soon as he picked up the phone, it began ringing in his hand. Looking at the screen, he saw that it was an unknown number, so he ignored it, sending the call to voicemail. He immediately texted Bomani, asking him to meet him at their spot right away.

***

DB stared at his reflection in the dull, scratched-up stainless steel mirror on the wall of the chilly holding cell for ten minutes straight. Deep inside, a part of him felt bad about agreeing to set up Bomani and the others, especially when he thought of all that they'd been through together over the five and a half years he'd known them. He was afraid that Bomani would be able to sense he wasn't being completely truthful about the drunk driving story.

DB had been convincing himself for the past twenty-six hours or so that Bomani only cared about himself and his homicidal sister. In his slightly distraught state, he told himself that if Bomani were in his position, he would throw him and Shiesty under the bus to save himself and Sentrice.

"Fuck that! It's either me or them!" DB told the sad reflection staring back at him.

DB had blown a lot of money on gay fantasy hookups and, most recently, paid a plastic surgeon to do his gender reassignment surgery. The deal that the detective and her captain laid out in front of him, in exchange for his cooperation, would give him a new start in his true form. DB could finally stop living a macho and Machiavellian charade.

The loud bang from Hermon letting the trapdoor in the holding cell's heavy steel door slam shut snapped DB out of his daydream of becoming the woman that he was on the inside.

"Are you almost ready? Because we're ready when you are," Hermon inquired through the opening.

***

"Bro, everything you need is here, so you don't need to go outside for nothing," Bomani said, then remembered seeing Shiesty's car parked out front. "Bro, move yo' car first, then come back and lay low."

"Okay, but then what, bro? You know I can't just stay in this bitch forever. I'ma need some bread to get the fuck outta Dodge, my nigga."

"We're not there yet, bro. You didn't do shit, so let me go holla at my lawyer and see what he say he can do 'bout this shit you're in."

Shiesty agreed, and with that, both of them went and got to work on their assigned tasks. Shiesty put on a hoodie and dark shades before going out and moving his car. Bomani decided it would be best to follow him so he could give him a ride back to the house safely.

Chapter 21

Being the last one in the home where they'd just botched a home invasion/kidnapping, Jaheim took a moment to do a quick search of the place to see if he could find anything that would tell him Shiesty was indeed one of the members of the team he was sent out to put an end to. After coming up with nothing more than what he already knew going in, Jaheim collected his thoughts while at the same time praying that nobody had paid attention to the noise of the shooting that had taken place inside the home. With nothing more to be done, he decided it was time to put space between himself and the bodies.

He tried to make it outside and to his vehicle unseen. Peeking out of the front entrance door, he made eye contact with a nosy neighbor coming up to the house to investigate the gunfire he'd heard when he stepped out on his porch to smoke.

"Hey! Stop!" the man yelled at the unfamiliar face peeking out of his neighbor's home. "Don't move!"

Jaheim did not listen. He promptly did the opposite of what he was being ordered to do. He slammed the door, then ran out the way that Shiesty and his guy had gone to get away. Not far behind, Jaheim heard the neighbor yell for him to stop once more, and again Jaheim didn't pay him no mind—not even when he heard the two warning shots the man fired in the air. He just kept moving, sprinting across the backyard, through the neighboring yard, and toward the front of the house. The only thing on his mind was getting as far away from there as fast as he could—and doing it possibly unharmed.

Suddenly, Jaheim was tackled to the ground by a second man who came at him from the opposite direction.

"I got him!"

Jaheim's foot crashed into his face, instantly hushing him up and putting him to sleep. Jaheim jumped to his feet and was met by the man he'd seen coming up the porch.

"Stop! Don't move!"

Moving swiftly, Jaheim kicked him in the balls. Instantly, the fool doubled over, and Jaheim kneed him in the face several hard times, knocking the fight right out of him. The neighbor tried to raise his gun but was too close and too slow. Jaheim grabbed the arm holding the gun and twisted it until he heard it snap. Without waiting to see who was up next, he took off running again.

Jaheim stopped just a few houses from his car. The winded thug pressed himself up against the side of a house, holding his side and once again praying that no one had seen which way he went. After a few minutes with nobody following him, he walked out of hiding, trying his best not to run and attract the attention of the police who'd made it on the scene. He half-limped to his car. Once inside safely, he immediately pulled out into traffic and exhaled.

When he hit the corner, he thought that someone might have taken down his plate number. He immediately switched vehicles when he made it home, making sure to remove his back plate so he could report it stolen if the police contacted him about it.

Next, he went back to Sentrice's place and fed her a story about getting jumped by a group of teenagers his friend had gotten into it with.

"No vital organs seem to be hurt," Sentrice informed Jaheim as she felt around his stomach with her fingers. "And no bones seem to be broken either. If they were, you'd be in a lot more pain than you are now, and I wouldn't be able to press on it like this. But I could be wrong, Mr. Tough Guy."

"That's good enough for me. Later, you're going to have to tell me how you know this stuff, but right now, just please get me whatever you got for pain and let me lay here for a while," he said, faking the level of his pain.

Sentrice shook her head, then skipped over to the bathroom cabinet, pulled out a bottle of acetaminophen, and handed him the small pill bottle, telling him to take two of them with a full glass of water. Jaheim walked to the sink, took four capsules, and washed them down with a glass of water from the bathroom sink.

"Here, let me run you a nice hot bath so you can soak in it. It'll help with the pain," she suggested. Not waiting for him to answer, she turned on the water in her double-wide jacuzzi tub.

Somewhere around fifteen minutes later, sitting in the relaxing, massaging bubbles enveloped in smooth R&B music, Sentrice couldn't stop thinking of how perfect Jaheim was for her. There was nothing she could find about him that didn't turn her on or make her second-guess the choices she was making to be with him.

"Do you love me?" she asked, taking a sip from her glass of chilled Dolce & Gabbana wine.

"I think I love everything about you," Jaheim replied, briefly pausing the foot massage he was giving her. "Honestly, I just realized that when you were the first person I thought of getting to after I got jumped," he admitted, restarting his rubbing of her foot.

"Is that so?" She took another sip. "That puts me right up there with your mother," she giggled.

"You're laughing, but it's kinda true. Only my auntie is the one who raised me most of my life, so it puts you right up there with her."

"No, I'm not laughing like that. It just makes me feel special...I had a talk with my brother about you."

"Oh yeah?" Jaheim asked, switching feet. "How did that go?"

"Better than I thought it would." She smiled. "I had to get him to accept me as a woman as well as his baby sister. He did threaten to kill you if you hurt me or allowed anything to hurt me, though."

"And there it goes . . . That's fair," he chuckled. "Did you tell him that you're not moving to Georgia with him?"

"Yeah, I told him." She took a sip from her glass. "At first, he wasn't really feeling it, but the more we spoke, the more he began to accept it. I guess he could see that I'm happy for the first time in a long time."

While Sentrice spoke, Jaheim's mind was elsewhere, trying to figure out what went wrong on the mission. He couldn't wait until he got his hands on the ones behind the robberies so he could focus on the beauty in front of him.

Once the two were out of the tub, Jaheim checked his phone to see if he had missed calls or messages. When he turned back around, he saw Sentrice standing behind him with her hands behind her back and a smile on her face.

"Close your eyes. I have a surprise for you."

"Huh?"

"Close your eyes, baby," she said excitedly.

Jaheim closed his eyes and waited until she told him he could open them.

When he did, he saw a beautiful diamond-encrusted Dior watch in her hand. "Surprise!" she shouted, extending the box toward him.

He looked down at the diamond watch with shock on his face. The watch was a deep gold with Dior printed across its face in diamonds, telling him it was expensive.

"I can't accept this."

"Sure you can," she smiled. "Here, try it on so I can see how it looks on you."

"This thing had to have cost you a small bank," he said as he slid the watch down on his wrist, then rotated it back and forth for her, watching the diamonds flicker in the light.

She had taken the watch off one of the men before she'd killed him, so she wouldn't lose any sleep over giving it to Jaheim. She felt that giving him such an expensive gift would show that she loved him for real.

Jaheim was about to reply when his cellphone started vibrating in his hand. He looked at the screen and saw Chief Ken's name on the screen.

"Hold on, baby. I have to take this," he said, walking off to answer his phone. "Yeah?"

"You have to go, don't you?" Sentrice asked in a pouty voice.

"Yeah, I do, baby, but I won't be long. I'll be right back," he promised.

The ringing of Sentrice's phone grabbed her attention. She looked down at her screen and saw the name of a guy she'd used for sex a time or two before. Annoyed, she rolled her eyes, pressed ignore, and turned her attention back to Jaheim.

"Baby, can't you just stay for a little while longer?" she whined. "Just tell whoever it is that you're hurt."

"I can't, baby," he said, pulling her close for a hug. Then he kissed her on the forehead and went to get dressed.

Sentrice stood wrapped in a fluffy terry cloth robe with a disappointed look on her face when her cellphone rang again. She was getting ready to hit ignore again but paused when she saw her brother's name on the screen.

"Hello?"

"You busy right now?"

"No, not really anymore. Why? Whud up?"

"Meet me at my crib in an hour," Bomani barked, then ended the call before she could question him more.

Chapter 22

After being told by the no-nonsense detective duo that the $12,900 bail for his drunk driving and criminal damage to property charges had been paid, DB was shown a photo and asked to confirm that the man at the cashier's window was Bomani.

"I don't know who this is. Are y'all sure that this is the right photo?" DB asked, pushing the photo back across the table.

"Yes, I'm sure!" Hermon exclaimed, meeting Lont's questioning eyes. "I printed it off the video myself."

"DB, you wouldn't be trying to renege on us now, would you?" Lont inquired as she stood up from her seat and crossed the room to the exit.

"No, I'm being straight up wit' y'all. I ain't ever seen that guy in the photo before, but that don't mean Bomani didn't send him down here to pay the bail. You heard him say that he'll be here to pick me up, so you'll see him then. I'm not tryna play y'all, I swear!"

"I believe you," Lont said, opening the door. "The photo was taken two hours ago, so I think you need to get down to release staging before you miss that ride."

DB was escorted down to release staging, where the techs returned his cellphones, now all wired for sound. Before heading out to the elevator, DB went into the restroom and gave himself a once-over in the mirror to make sure his nervousness wasn't showing, then headed out of the building.

Outside, he surveyed the congested streets in front of the jail, looking for his ride home as well as the detectives he knew would be following them. DB was wondering if it was the double-parked Speedway Delivery truck or the ABC Plumbing van that concealed the detectives when he heard Bomani's horn blaring, pulling his attention to his heavily tinted SUV. DB took a deep breath, then briskly walked over to the vehicle.

"I'm glad you came, Bo," he said, climbing into the passenger seat and closing the door.

"You say that like you thought I wouldn't," Bomani retorted with a frown as he merged back into traffic. "Now, please tell me what in the hell happened."

DB slightly turned in the seat, unconsciously scanning Bomani's right hand that lay on his thigh for his gun. DB told himself in his head to get it together, then told a modified version of what happened the night of his arrest, making sure to leave out the part about the shootout with the police where he'd shot a cop and then took the others on a short wild chase. Instead, he fed him a quick story that he was speeding down the street when suddenly a dog ran out in front of him, causing him to lose control, jump the curb, and crash his car into a porch.

"Bo, I need your help with this," he said in a serious tone. "I don't know what to do. They took my money but haven't said anything about it except that it's being held for review by a judge because of the amount."

"What the fuck do that mean?" Bomani questioned. For all the years he'd known DB, he'd never been the type of driver to get spooked by a dog in the street, so he knew DB must've really been drunk.

"I don't fuckin' know."

"Why didn't you call me when it happened?"

"I was embarrassed, to be honest." DB dropped his head, then said, "I tried to call Shiesty as soon as I got to a phone, but he didn't answer. What's going on with him?" he asked, taking the conversation off himself for a bit.

"Ahhh, Shiesty got himself in some shit too," Bomani said, shaking his head. "I was with him when you called. I don't know. He said somethin' about some niggas runnin' up in his crib on some robbery shit. Here, call him on his burner and let him tell you." He passed DB his cellphone so he could get Shiesty's number to call him. "I guess ole Gary finna have to show me what all that bread I been giving him over the years bought me."

"Bo, I'm fucked up."

"What you mean you fucked up? What you been doing with all yo money?"

"You know I've been helping pay my mother's bills, and I been paying for medical shit," DB explained. "I was counting on that money they took to put me back in the green."

"Damn, man!" Bomani exclaimed as he made a left turn onto Lake Drive. "I got you, but I want my bread back when you get yours back from them people," he said, glancing over at DB, who quickly diverted his eyes down at his phone in his lap.

"You got that . . . But I know that shit gon' take some time for them to get back, and I still need to take care of everything."

"So, what do you need me to do?"

"I was wondering if we could hit another lick besides what you got planned for us? Just something quick and easy—maybe even one of the spots we hit already?"

Bomani chuckled at the suggestion but took a moment to consider what his friend was saying.

"D, I plan things out for a reason, and you know I don't like to do anything on the spur of the moment. So if you need some cash on top of me taking care of the lawyer until we can do this last move, I got you."

"Bo, I know you getting ready to move and everything, so I don't wanna tap into that and hold y'all up."

With the way DB was talking, if he was anybody else, Bomani would've been suspicious. But he had been dealing with DB for years, so he looked past his friend's persistence about doing another robbery with him.

"Listen, bro-bro, I got you. We are like family, remember? And family always supposed to look out for family."

As soon as the sincere words left Bomani's lips, DB immediately felt the sting of regret for selfishly agreeing to set him up. He wondered what he could do now that he was at the point of no return. Even if he wanted to back out of the deal, it was too late. He knew the detectives would make it their business to tell Bomani and the others what he'd tried to do to save himself.

"Are you sure that won't be too much on you with you leaving and all?"

"It's never too much for family," Bomani replied, turning into the office building's parking lot.

"I really appreciate this. You know if there's anything you need me to do for you, all you gotta do is ask."

"All I need you to do is to look after my sister when I leave."

"I thought she was going with you?"

Bomani shook his head and pushed the gearshift into park.

"It's time for her to grow up. But I can count on you to have her back, right?"

DB nodded *yes*.

"Thanks. I really mean that. And, bro, I'ma give you a lil extra out of my cut of the cash so you won't have to worry much. Now let's go," Bomani said and then got out.

"Fuck!" DB cursed under his breath. He knew that once Bomani's mind was set on something, it was near impossible to get him to change it.

DB followed him into the fancy office building, no longer feeling the intense resentment toward his friend that he felt when he made the deal with the detectives. Now, he felt the need to figure another way out—fast.

Chapter 23

The studious Detective Lont sat in the back of the delivery van alongside Hermon, who was holding a high-powered camera. They were both praying to get a few identifying shots of Bomani, the crafty leader of the deadly robbery crew, when he arrived to pick up his driver and friend. Bomani had already slipped through their grasp once by sending someone else to the cashier's window to post the bond for their new informant, DB. DB had described Bomani to them as a tall, handsome man who's usually dressed business casual.

"So, what have you learned about this Bomani guy?" Hermon asked, snapping a few shots of the scenery outside of the jail.

"Nothing much. I can't find anything on him in our database," Lont shrugged. "All I know is that he's a dangerous man who needs to be off the streets."

"Why can't we arrest this guy today?" asked the young backup officer who was watching DB's tracker.

"Because we need DB to get him to talk about the next job he has planned so we can catch him and the rest of the team red-handed. I don't wanna give any of them a way out of the life behind bars that they all deserve," Lont explained.

"Heads up, I think we got some action!" Hermon announced.

Lont looked up and noticed an SUV pull over to the curb in front of her informant. Lont knew from the dark tinted windows that this was their suspect.

"That's him," she vociferated, encouraging her gung-ho partner next to her to snap several pictures of DB walking over and climbing into the SUV, still hoping to catch a shot of the man behind the wheel on film.

Once their informant disappeared behind the glass, Lont quickly covered her ears with headphones, hoping DB could get Bomani to incriminate himself on the wire while her partner casually merged into traffic a few cars behind the SUV. Hermon wasn't worried about losing sight of them because of the GPS on their informant's phones that DB didn't know about. Being able to stay a nice distance behind the suspects gave them room to focus on building their case.

***

DB followed Bomani to the freshly polished reception desk, where a sexy strawberry blonde sat pecking away on the keyboard while simultaneously talking on the phone. DB felt a light nip of jealousy when the woman flirtatiously waved and smiled at his secret crush.

"Hey, how are you doing, Madison?" Bomani greeted the receptionist by name once she'd completed her call.

"I'll be great if you're here to take me out to a late lunch?"

"Don't tell me that you've worked through your break again?" She nodded yes, adding a little pout to her lips.

"Luv, you can't be killin' yourself for these asses here. One of these days I'ma take you out and never bring you back."

"Do you promise?"

"I don't make those. I let my actions speak my truth," he replied with a wink and a smile, then requested to see his lawyer. "Can you tell Rasey that I'm here, please?" Bomani

91

asked, placing a $20 bill on the desk. "Here's my raincheck on lunch, but maybe dinner one day soon?"

"I'll be waiting," she said, then immediately went back to pecking away on the keyboard again. Moments later, she said, "Mr. Rosenberg is expecting you."

"Thank you!" Bomani said and then instructed DB to fall back until he called for him before heading to the office at the end of the hall.

When DB saw Bomani enter Rosenberg's office, leaving him in the waiting area of the lobby, DB's nerves started getting the best of him.

"Fuck, fuck, fuck!" he cursed loudly.

The realness of what he was doing was too intense for him to fully comprehend. If Bomani somehow found out that he was wired up and working for the cops, he could only imagine what Bomani would do to him. Having serious second thoughts, DB put some distance between himself and the ear-hustling receptionist before pulling out his cellphone and calling the detective.

"We need more," Lont immediately said when she answered the call.

"What you mean you need more?" DB snapped.

"He didn't admit to robbing anything, nor did he give us any information on this mysterious next job he has planned. We have nothing real on him," Hermon said, letting DB know he was on speakerphone. "If you want to walk away free, then you better get me something I can work with."

"I'm trying!" Frustrated, DB hung up and went in search of a vending machine to get something to drink. *Fuck this shit! Whatever money Bo gives me, I'ma use it to go on the run. I'll have a new look soon anyway*, he thought to himself.

When Bomani strolled into the office, just as he expected, Rosenberg sat leaned back in his plush black leather chair with his feet kicked up on his desk, talking on his cellphone while flipping a cigar between his fat fingers.

"Good to see you, Bo!" he greeted, smiling after ending his call. Rosenberg stood up to shake Bomani's hand before motioning for him to take a seat.

"Good to see you too, man," Bomani replied, sitting down. "So, how's DB's case looking?"

Rosenberg nodded. "The good news is that it looks like a simple review of financial verification issues which usually ends in a fine of some sort."

"That's fine. What type of fine?"

"No more than ten percent of the seized amount."

"He should be good with that. Hell, somethin' is better than nothin'. Before I call him in here, I need you to keep me posted on his case. I wanna know things when you know them, 'cause something don't sit right wit' me about it."

"Since you're the one paying the bill, I can do that for you. Bo, out of curiosity, what about it isn't sitting right with you?"

"I just think that the Feds should be involved because of the money, that's all."

"Got you. I'll keep my eye out for any snooping by the Feds and let you know immediately if something pops up."

With that assurance, Bomani sent DB a text summoning him into the office. When he arrived, Bomani left them alone to talk, deciding to use the time to lock down a date with Madison.

Chapter 24

Leaving the meeting with the lawyer, DB really felt that he needed to get even further away from the situation he'd put himself in. Just from the conversation with Rosenberg, he could tell that the little fat man was very good at his job, which only told DB that there was a good chance of him finding out about his deal with the detectives.

"Man, I can't let you break yourself on me. Not when I'm here and can help you get it. Hell, we can do it—just the two of us," DB suggested, beginning his second round of campaigning for them to hit another of the cartel's cash spots before they did the farewell job that Bomani had planned out for them.

"Bro, I said I got you. It's not a problem, really. See, what you don't know is that yo' boy here recently invested some money with the owner of Shoreline Investments. It's the same place that stars like R. Kelly and Nitty Baggz use," Bomani humbly bragged, then said, "All I gotta do is call my man and let him know that I'ma need to make an early withdrawal of 60 or 70 geez—or take it out as a loan on what I invested."

"What's wrong, Bo? Did getting me out make things tight for you?" DB asked, impressed that his friend hadn't just been burning through his money like him and the others. For as long as DB had known Bomani, he'd always been well-organized and always seemed to be thinking steps ahead of everyone he dealt with. "Bo, I gotta admit, I'm impressed."

"Thanks! But like I said to you earlier, it's not just about me—it's about us as a whole," Bomani said, picking up the phone and dialing the number to Shoreline Investments.

DB sat back and began to think about Sentrice and what the detectives actually said they wanted—the shooter. He was trying to come up with a plan where he could give them her and Shiesty in exchange for them letting him and Bomani walk away. DB was putting a scheme together when he noticed an expression of confusion on his friend's face. Right away, DB's mind went to the lawyer. He was thinking Rosenberg had somehow found him out already and was now telling Bomani.

"What's wrong?" he inquired, not wanting to do anything stupid because of his paranoia.

"It says that the number has been disconnected," Bomani answered, trying the number again. "It's still sayin' the muthafuckin' number is disconnected."

"Do you have another number that you can reach somebody there at?"

"Yeah, I got the office number and my investor's wife's number," Bomani said, then dialed Shoreline Investments directly. Three rings later, his call was answered by a polite feminine voice asking how she could help him. Bomani demanded to talk to Mr. Nash and was informed that Mr. Nash had taken a vacation and did not say when he would be returning. Again, the polite voice asked if she could be of some assistance. This time, Bomani explained what he needed done.

She took his name, and he could hear what he believed to be her tapping a few keys on a keyboard. "What the fuck you mean I no longer have an account with you?... Bitch, you better find somebody that can tell me something! . . . Hello? Hello?" Bomani pulled out of traffic and parked.

DB saw the shock and disgusted expression on his face and knew it was all bad.

"Whud up, Bo, talk to me," he said, slipping the bugged cellphone out of his pocket and placing it beneath his leg to try and give them some privacy from the snooping detectives, who he knew were hanging on every word being said. Since DB's new personal mission was to save Bo from them, he didn't need them hearing anymore of what was going on.

"Fuck! Fuck! Fuck! Somebody tell me this is a joke," Bomani exclaimed, dialing another number. "Where in the hell is he?" he barked into the phone at Mrs. Nash.

"Bomani, I've been waiting for your call. Eric found out about us spending that evening together and went ballistic. He beat me and then stormed out of the house. He said he was going to kill you," she distraughtly explained.

"So you're telling me that he took my money and ran off? Or what are you saying, because I'm still standing, but I can't find my bread."

"I don't know what he took from you, but he has locked me out of all of our accounts, so I believe that he did take your money as well."

"Bitch, you listen to me because I'm only gonna ask you nicely once. Where can I find him?"

"We got a summer home in Florida. That's the only place I can think of him being. I'll text you the address. Bo, do me a favor and make him hurt for me when you catch him."

With that agreement set, they ended the call, and she sent Bomani the address and home alarm code to the Florida home.

"How much money did you invest with this dirtbag?" DB inquired as Bomani pulled back into traffic real calm-like. DB knew whenever he got calm like this in the middle of a crisis, nothing good was going to come to the person Bomani was angry with.

"Two mill."

"Two mill! Damn, that's a lot of money, Bo. I hate to be whoever took it right now," DB said, shaking his head with a little whistle of amazement.

Bomani said nothing more. He only focused on the road as he drove DB home. Every now and then, he would shake his head and mumble something that DB couldn't understand. DB knew he wasn't talking to him and also knew to just let him be right now. What he didn't know was that Bomani had invested his and his sister's entire life savings with Shoreline. Every cent that he'd risked his and Sentrice's life for was gone.

"That was all of me and Sen's money, bro . . . Fuck that, I'ma need that back!"

"Bo, if you need me to go with you to handle this, you know I'm wit' you."

"Nah, I'm good. Me and Shiesty will handle it. I don't need you to fuck up that bail money on a humbug."

A short while later, they were stopped in front of DB's home. "I'll call you in a couple days," Bomani said before DB got out of the truck and headed inside.

Bomani sat there double-parked for a moment, then banged on the steering wheel a few times before pulling off again. The feeling of possibly losing all of him and his sister's money had his thoughts racing and his blood boiling. He was mad at himself for being stupid enough to mix business with pleasure. When Mrs. Nash booked that room for him to stay another night after having a threesome with her and her husband, he knew he should've passed, but he was feeling himself and trusted that she knew how to cover her tracks. Now he saw that he was wrong.

He didn't know if he would get all of his money back, but he knew he was going to get something—and that Eric Nash was going to pay whatever the balance was in blood. Then he planned to circle back and get even more out of the wife before sending her to join her lousy spouse.

Chapter 25

I might slap da shit outta a bitch / Make her know I ain't playin' around / I rock Prada, fuck wit' ball'z / That be movin' pounds / I made a nigga cash me out / These bitches gon' fuck for free doe.

Sentrice pulled up to her brother's house and killed the music. She was so curious to find out what was so important that he called her to come over the way he had. So many crazy thoughts ran through her mind on the drive over. She thought that maybe the cartel had somehow found out who they were, or maybe the police had someone who could identify them. She quickly dismissed that idea because if that was the case, Bomani definitely would've come and got her from wherever she was instead of calling her to his house.

To be safe, Sentrice slipped her gun in her pocket, just in case she had to make a quick getaway or save her brother from whatever brought on the strange call. She nonchalantly walked to the front door, scanning all of the shadows before she let herself in with the key she had to her brother's place.

As soon as she stepped inside, Bomani and Shiesty were both standing in his living room, talking and smoking with very serious, no-nonsense expressions on their faces. The first thing Sentrice noticed was that DB wasn't there with them, then she noticed the tacky way Shiesty was dressed. Instead of the usual high-end brand names that he wore daily, she saw that he was dressed in work clothes: black jeans, a black hoodie, and a pair of black Air Force Ones.

"Hey, what's up? Where's DB?" she questioned as she stepped further into the room where they were.

"He's at the crib. Since he's out on bail, I told him to sit tight."

"Out on bail? What da fuck!"

"Oh shit, my bad, sis. So much bullshit got thrown at me today I just forgot to tell you about all this crazy shit. I ain't got time now because me and Shiesty gotta go to Florida tonight to handle some business. Sen, listen, if you don't hear from either of us by tomorrow night, I want you to do a search for us down there. But don't bring yo' hot-head ass down there. You hear me?"

"Naw! Hell naw! Bo, you gotta give me more than that shit you just said!"

"Listen to me, Sen. I need you to do what I asked you to do. If things don't go right, you and DB are the ones that'll have to come get us. I don't have time for your shit right now," Bomani barked at her.

"My shit? Bo, you talkin' like y'all finna go to war down there and shit. I'm your sister, and you're all I got, so I deserve to know what this is about," she protested, arms folded, standing her ground.

"I need you to take us to the airport anyway, so I'll fill you in on the way."

The drive to the airport was an emotional one, to say the least. Sentrice wasn't sure what brought on all the sudden bad luck surrounding them. As she listened to Shiesty telling the story of what went on with him, she wondered if it was a sign of what was to come for everyone when her brother broke off from them and moved.

Bomani knew his sister well enough to know that when she was as quiet as she was during the trip to the airport, it meant she'd slipped into her murderous mind state. So when she argued the point that she had the right to go get her money back just as much as he did, Shiesty didn't protest. He stayed out of it because he knew Sentrice believed the only way she'd know her brother was in good hands down in Florida was if it was her finger on the trigger that had his back.

By the time they'd arrived at Mitchell Field, all he could do was wish the siblings luck and pray they made it back from Florida in one piece.

"Be careful down there, and send me a text as soon as y'all land and as soon as y'all handle that shit. If you don't, I'ma be on the next thing smokin'," Shiesty said, getting behind the wheel of Bomani's SUV.

"I got you, bro-bro, but since you stayin' back, that don't mean be out in these streets. You gotta stay low 'til you and Rosie go handle yo shit," Bomani told him as Sentrice put her gun in his hand before they let him go and headed inside the airport.

"Bo, I know this ain't a social trip we're going down here on, but I was just thinkin' . . ."

"Yeah, yeah, I know what you were thinkin'. I called her."

"You did?"

"Sen, who else I know down there? She's picking us up from the airport with the stuff we need. Well, me up. She don't know your pushy ass comin' with me."

"It don't matter, Domonique always got room for me," Sentrice said, smiling from ear to ear at the thought of seeing her friend, who is also Bomani's ex-girlfriend. "Bo, don't start nothin' with her when we get there, please?"

"I'm just going down there to get what was taken from me. That's it, that's all. She the one who left, so I don't got time for her either," he promised, even though he really did want to see Domonique as much as his sister did.

They collected their tickets and passed the time trying to figure out who'd run up on Shiesty until it was time to board the plane. On the plane, Bomani gave Sentrice the window seat without fuss because the only thing on his mind was getting their money back and killing Eric Nash for thinking he could rob a robber. He had already made up his mind that he was going to let Sentrice loose when they found him.

The plane landed smoothly in Florida. As soon as the wheels touched down, memories of the last time the two of them were there came flooding back to Bomani's mind, as well as the ones of when he first met Domonique and moved here to Milwaukee with her. Bomani had to smile at his sister's excitement as he kept pace with her quick steps through the small crowd of people who dared to fly in the pandemic.

They exited the airport and were met by the lovely Domonique's smiling face. The two women crashed into each other's arms in tearful joy as they hugged.

"Gurl, I didn't know you were comin'! Look at you!" Domonique said once they broke their embrace.

"You know I wouldn't pass up a chance to see my big sis!"

"You two can catch up in the car on the way to the motel," Bomani said, trying to hide his excitement to see her.

"Motel? No, you guys are staying with us," Domonique said, giving him a brief half-hug before sashaying around the front of her GMC Acadia and getting behind the wheel.

"Who is us?" Bomani inquired as he slid into the backseat of the truck he'd bought for her four years ago when they were together. "Niq, who is us?" he asked again, getting a bit jealous because of the baby's car seat that was in the back with him.

"Hey, hey! Y'all two please don't start," Sentrice spoke up. "We're only going to be here a few hours."

"Yeah, Bo, don't start. If not for you, just let us enjoy our time together," Domonique said, then pulled into traffic. "Everything y'all gon' need is in the bag."

Bomani picked up the pink-and-white duffel bag with pictures of the *Frozen* movie characters printed on it and peeked inside. In the bag, he found two Glock 20s with four extended 30-round clips, ammo, and a box of black latex gloves. He nodded his approval to Domonique, who was watching him through the rearview mirror.

With nothing more to say, he rested his head back against the headrest and closed his eyes, trying his best to figure out who the man in her life was. He listened to the sweet sound of Domonique's voice as she and Sentrice chatted about everything—from Sentrice's new boyfriend to the daughter Domonique had left at the babysitter's.

Chapter 26

Jaheim rode in silence the entire fifteen-minute drive to his friend's apartment building. His mind was on his friend that he'd accidentally shot because he knew it was only a matter of time before the police came looking for him because of his blood on the scene. He wasn't worried about him talking to the cops, but to be safe, Jaheim made a mental note to go and drop him off some cash for his troubles.

Concealing his gun on his waist, Jaheim hopped out of his car and entered the building, saluting a few of the guys he knew that were hanging out front of the place. Inside, he walked past the elevator that had a fresh "out of order" sign taped to its door. Seeing it, he was glad that he didn't have to leave off of the bottom floor because he wasn't in the mood to climb multiple flights of stairs. He stopped in front of the last door on the left and knocked heavily on the door.

Within minutes, a malefic-looking teen snatched open the door. Jaheim ignored him as he pushed past the young fool and entered the apartment. The inside of the unit resembled more of a pharmacy than it did a home. As he made his way through the place, he saw that there were all types of pharmaceuticals in the spacious apartment—everything from medical-grade morphine patches to vials of the COVID-19 vaccine. There was even a table of heroin where men and women were hard at work mixing and packaging it up like true-life pharmacists.

Jaheim's journey ended when he entered a room where two goons stood posted with their guns visible beside Chief Ken, who was seated at a table in front of twin currency counters, counting his cash. He stood and greeted Jaheim with a handshake.

"Sit and rap with me for a minute," Chief Ken motioned to an open seat at the table.

"CK, is that vaccine you got in there the real thing?" Jaheim inquired as he sat down.

"Hell yeah, it's real. Since you my nigga, I'll have one of them bitches in there hook you up with a shot for free."

"Nawl, man, I'm good cuz. Shouldn't you have that shit in a freezer so it won't go bad?"

"Nawl, that's that new Johnson & Johnson shit that don't need all that super-cold shit—and it's one and done. That shit ain't even made it to the States yet. Fam, I'm telling you it's all good. We all got ours, and I'm feeling great, fam. COVID-proof like Superman in this bitch!" Chief Ken said, showing him a Band-Aid on his arm where he'd gotten his shot. A few others in the room showed off their arms as well. "My nigga, I've been clockin' like fifty geez a vial with this doctor I be fuckin' with who likes to powder his nose with that flake. Fam, life's sweet!"

"Yeah, I heard about it . . . I'ma trust you on it. Plus, I grew up fuckin' with the Johnsons from baby powder to baby oil, so yeah, go'n tell 'em to come hook me up," Jaheim said, reading the label on an empty vial that was lying on the table amidst stacks of cash. "CK, you know I don't like being in here with all this, so what up? Why you call me over here?" he asked while rolling up his sleeve so a cute short chubby female could give him the shot.

"I just thought I'd tell you in person that we caught two of them bitch-ass niggas that ran up in my spot and killed my BM."

"How you do that? And where the muthafuckaz at now?"

"Fam, you know how broke niggas get when they come into some bread—all out flashy, bragging and shit. Loose lips sink ships, so now them bitches worm food somewhere—I don't know."

"Shit, I wonder if one of 'em was that nigga that got away from me."

"I don't know, but if you run into him again, handle that shit for me, and I got you. I just had to let you know what was up because I can't keep letting that shit control me the way it was. It got to making me miss too much bread. So, as of right now, I'm focused on getting it up—and nothing else."

"I feel you," Jaheim said to him, even though he could see that the big man was still very much hurting inside by the pain in his eyes. "But my nigga, you didn't have to call me over here for you to tell me this shit. You could've just told me to fall back over the phone."

"You know I don't do much talkin' on that. Plus, I wanna give you a lil somethin' for your troubles on top of that shot. I know you said for me not to worry about it, but I really appreciate how you came ASAP and got right on it. So take this and go have some fun." Chief Ken placed a nice wad of cash in front of Jaheim. "That's five. Now, before you try to refuse, know that I'm going to be offended if you don't take it."

"Well, I ain't trying to offend nobody. Good lookin', big homie," Jaheim collected the money and stuffed it in his jacket pocket. He immediately planned to pass it on to the guy he shot, so it was right on time.

"It's no biggie. Now, I know you said that you ain't tryna sit, but I'm curious to know what happened that one of 'em got away from you. That ain't like you."

After telling a quick version of how things went down in the house, being sure to leave out the part where he shot his own man, Jaheim stood up out of his seat, indicating that his story was over and that he'd had enough of sitting in the spot.

Him and Chief Ken shook hands again, and he left back out the way he came, only vaccinated and five thousand dollars richer than he was when he walked in.

But the thing that puzzled him was the part his homie said about the guys they caught being out in the streets bragging. From how they moved on the video of the robbery that he'd gotten from Chief Ken, he seriously doubted that anyone from the crew he was looking for would be so careless. Even the guy that had gotten away from him wasn't out there, nor did he even know if he really was a part of the crew or not.

But if Chief was happy, then so was he happy for him.

Jaheim got back in his car, and before he headed back to Sentrice's place, he stopped at Love's Liquor Store. He sent Sentrice a text telling her that he was on his way and asking her if she needed him to pick up anything on his way. That's when she responded, telling him that she had a family emergency that she had to attend to out of town with her brother and that she would be back in two days to make it up to him.

With that disappointing news, he decided to head on over to his guy's house so he could give him the money, smoke, and chill while thinking of where he really was trying to take things with Sentrice. Jaheim smiled, admiring the sparkle of his new watch under the liquor store sign light.

Chapter 27

On the way to the address where Bomani believed Eric was staying, his mind was moving a hundred thousand miles a second. He was reeling from Domonique telling him that her two-year-old daughter was his child. The little girl wasn't at her place when they got there from the airport, so he'd only gotten to see photos of her. Domonique told him that she wanted to tell him first, without their daughter being there, in case he didn't want to have anything to do with her or their child. From the photos of the little girl, it was hard for Bomani to deny her because she looked just like Sentrice when she was about her age.

Overwhelmed by the bomb that had been dropped on his life, Bomani couldn't think of anything else to do but hold his child, so he instructed Domonique to take them to do what they came down there to do so he could get it over with and meet his little girl—and Sentrice could meet her niece for the first time in person. Unlike her brother, Sentrice knew that Domonique had a child; she just didn't know that the little girl she'd *FaceTimed* with was her niece. Sentrice didn't tell her brother about the child because she was asked not to, and since Domonique was the second most important person in her life, she respected her wishes.

Domonique pulled over outside of the Nash residence, parking in the shadows to give them cover.

"Y'all be careful!" Domonique said, locking eyes with Bomani.

Bomani could see in her eyes that he wasn't the only one struggling with the emotions that he'd locked away years ago. He grinned and winked at her before pulling his mask up over his face, then grabbing his gun and quickly stepping out of the truck. Sentrice was right behind him, stone-faced and ready. Outside the front of the house, the two of them split up. Bomani made his way to the front door and entered the unlock code provided to him by Mrs. Nash. When the lock clicked open, he sent the code by text to his sister, who was waiting for his go order in the rear of the house.

Bomani entered the plantation-styled mansion cautiously, creeping deeper into the immaculately kept home. He followed the sound of bumping pop music coming from somewhere in the back of the place. The closer he got, the more voices he could hear. From the sound of it, Nash and friends were having a little party.

Peeking around the corner, Bomani spotted his target with ease. Eric Nash sat poolside at a patio table alongside the driver/bodyguard that Bomani had met when he first met Eric, and another man that went by the name Morty, who Bomani guessed was one of Eric's business partners.

"So, do you have any new business for us?" Morty asked, pulling a woman in a tiny two-piece swimsuit onto his lap.

"I'm working on these two new rap guys from Atlanta that just signed a recording deal and are now looking to invest a large sum of money with us. It'll be a piece of cake to lock them into a five-year contract," Eric answered.

The two of them had been playing the same game on people who didn't know any better for years and getting rich off of their scams. Eric and Morty were so good at it that they'd forgotten that what they were doing was illegal.

"Sounds good," Morty said, raising his glass of brandy to Eric before taking a sip.

"By the end of the month, we should pull in about ten million off of the NY setup, easy," Eric boasted. He loved to feel like he was the smartest person in the room, so he almost never took on any clients outside of the music industry or outlaws trying to clean up their dirty money.

"That's great news," Bomani exclaimed, stepping from the shadows with his gun hidden behind his back.

At the sight of the party crasher, the bodyguard instantly went for his gun that was laying on a tray table beside him but halted at the sound of Sentrice's gun cocking from behind him. That's when she ordered everyone to stay where they were and sit tight. Bomani snatched his mask off so Eric could see his face and know who was going to take his life.

"I'll take my money now—plus interest—if you don't mind," Bomani said, pointing his gun at Eric.

"Bomani? Hey man . . . Wh-wh-what are you doing here?" Eric stuttered.

"I just told you why I'm here. I tried calling your office and was told that you were on vacation, so I tried your cellphone and got no answer," Bomani said, unsmiling. "So I figured I'd drop by in person to hear your lame-ass explanation and collect my money."

"Bo, buddy, I was going to call you as soon as I returned and give you all of my new numbers," Eric lied, trying to act cool to hide his fear. "Me and my partner Morty here were just discussing our next moves for you."

"Is that right?" Bomani said, lowering his gun.

"Yeah, man, we were saying how smart it was of you to invest with us at this time because of the states being opened back up. In the next two years, your money sho—"

"Bitch, shut that bullshit up!" Sentrice snapped, cutting him off. "Give me my money, I want it now! All of it!" she said, stepping from the shadows behind them.

"Eric, meet my investment partner," Bomani said, nodding toward his sister.

"I'm going to need some time, Bo. That kind of cash isn't just lying around," Eric pleaded. "Getting it takes time."

"Wrong!" Sentrice exclaimed, then re-aimed at the sneaky bodyguard and squeezed the trigger twice, blowing him right out of his chair. His body made a big splash when it hit the pool.

Eric and his remaining guests watched in horror. The woman seated on Morty's lap instantly threw up. Quickly crossing the yard, Sentrice turned her gun on her as her next target.

"Eric, I don't think she's going to ask you again," Bomani told him.

"I have just about $350,000 upstairs in my safe. It's all I have here," Eric said, raising his hands in surrender. "Take it, it's yours, I swear I'll get you the rest."

"$350,000?" Bomani repeated. "Muthafucka, where's the rest of my money?"

"I don't have it. I used your money just the way I explained it would be used to you. So now all the money is currently tied up in those investments."

"I guess I look stupid to you, huh, Eric?" Bomani asked, then suddenly shot Morty in the head. Sentrice shot the woman because she started screaming. "All of your money isn't tied up in no fuckin' investments! So pick up your phone and unlock your bank accounts so your wife can have access to give me the rest of our fuckin' bread when we pay her a visit."

"How . . . Okay, okay!" Eric said, scrambling to pick up his cellphone. He punched in a series of numbers, then held it out so Bomani could see its screen. "There, it's done."

Pleased with what he saw on the screen, Bomani gave Eric a sad face and then nodded to Sentrice. Without questioning, she mercilessly massacred Eric's remaining guests.

Chapter 28

Shiesty knew Bomani had told him to lay low until the lawyer got back in touch with him, but he was going nuts just sitting around in the house doing nothing but waiting to hear from Rosenberg with the date and time he was setting up with the police that wanted to speak with him about the shooting that had taken place in his home. He was also waiting to hear from his friends, letting him know things went well for them down south. Shiesty almost had a heart attack when his cellphone rang. He saw it was DB calling and answered, hoping he could convince him to come over to keep him company.

"Shiesty, man, I need your help," DB said, sounding desperate.

"I hope it's something that don't require me to be out in the open because Bo and the lawyer told me to stay low."

"Nawl, you don't need to go nowhere. I just need you to help me convince Bo to let us hit another spot."

"Are you serious? You can't be serious right now," Shiesty exclaimed. "First off, my nigga, you know just as well as I know that Bo ain't going to agree to nothing on some ole spur-of-the-moment shit," he reminded him, then said, "Especially not when he got that lick already planned for us when he get back. He'd never risk messing up a big lick just cuz you on some thirsty shit."

"This ain't just some thirsty shit I'm on. Shiesty, you know me—I wouldn't be asking just because," he begged. "Man, I really need the money."

"I don't even wanna know what you on. And it's clear to me that you don't want me to know what it is either because you ain't told me. I'll run it by Bo and see what he says, but if I was you, I wouldn't get my hopes up," Shiesty said, giving in to his friend's request. "I gotta question for you on some whole other shit though."

"Whud up?" DB asked, a little nervous.

"How the fuck do you not see a whole house, my nigga?" he asked, laughing at him.

Relieved that he wasn't being questioned about his whereabouts, DB started laughing with him.

"I don't fuckin' know; it kinda just happened," DB replied. "Hey, it's like you always say: playas fuck up sometimes."

"You gonna have to stop drinking like that."

"You ain't gotta tell me twice. Two's my limit if I ain't where I'mma be for the night," DB assured him. "Call me when you hear something from Bo and Sen."

"I got you," Shiesty said, ending the call.

Something about DB's accident and his sudden need for extra cash didn't seem right. Shiesty didn't know what it was, but he planned on addressing it once everyone was together. With nothing else to do, he decided to sit out on the back porch so he wouldn't be easily seen if a police car just happened to be riding by. When he went out, he saw a little boy across the alley from him playing by himself in the garage while his sexy single mom—who Shiesty had been flirting with off and on in the past—set up the barbecue grill. It was obvious that she was trying to give the child some outdoor time from being a prisoner of the pandemic, which was just the way Shiesty felt at the moment. So, he said to hell with sitting alone and went over to give her a hand with things.

"Testing, testing. Rocket, can you hear me?" Shiesty said, speaking into one of the sets of little yellow two-way walkie-talkies that he'd given to the woman's seven-year-old son.

"Yeah, Star Lord, I can hear you loud and clear," the boy replied, loving the interactive way they were playing *Guardians of the Galaxy*. "What are you doing over there? Get to the control center and get us outta here."

"Rocket, I'm working on getting the shields down as fast as I can. You and Baby Groot just hang in there," Shiesty told him, playing along from the steps of his back porch, where he'd returned after getting the grill started for her.

The mother walked back into the garage carrying a tray of food and found her son there alone. She looked across the alley and saw Shiesty there pretending to be on another planet, talking to her son.

"Major, can I see that radio for a second?" she asked her son.

"I'm still playing with it, Mama," he said in a whiny voice.

"I'm not going to take it from you. I just wanna talk to Star Man over there right quick, and you can have it back."

"Okay, but Mama, his name is Star Lord," he corrected her, then handed her the two-way.

"Star Lord? Star Lord, come in," she said, playing along.

"Go for Star Lord, Queen Mama," Shiesty replied with a chuckle.

"Why don't you come back over here and sit down to eat with us, unless you have other plans?"

"No, no plans, Queen Mama. Star Lord is returning to home base," Shiesty replied, briskly walking back across the alley into the garage for dinner.

After having their fill of the home-cooked foods, the two of them played with her son until it was time for him to go to bed. Shiesty pretended to be on little Major's side when it came to trying to get her to allow him to stay up past his bedtime, when in truth, he was looking forward to some alone time with the mother.

"I see you got yourself a new car?" Shiesty said once the mother had returned from putting her son to bed.

"Yeah, thanks to your friend."

"What friend?"

"The one that got in the shootout with the police and crashed his Durango into that house the other night," she answered, handing him another beer.

"Shootout with the police?" he repeated, a little confused. "You're talkin' 'bout my guy DB, but he didn't get into no shootout with no police. His ass just got drunk and ran into a house."

"I don't know why he didn't tell you the part about the shootout, but that's what happened. I was on my way home early from work, sitting at the stoplight, when I noticed it was your friend's truck that the police had pulled over. I was going to record it because of all these damn police shootings," she said, shaking her head. "But then suddenly, your friend jumped out shooting at them, and I ducked behind the dashboard when they got to running behind him and shooting back. I didn't get none of that first part on my phone, but I did get when he crashed, then got out and passed out," she said as she pulled the video up on her phone for him to see.

Shiesty watched it twice from beginning to end. Even though he couldn't see the shootout on the video, the gunfire exchange could be heard. He asked her to send it to his phone so he could ask DB what really happened to him that night and why he didn't tell them about the shootout. Then it hit him that it might be the reason he was so desperate for money. On that thought, Shiesty decided to wait for Bomani's return to address it.

Chapter 29

Domonique opened her eyes later that morning only to find that she was alone. Panic immediately crept into her mind, making her wonder if Bomani had a change of heart sometime while she slept and didn't want the responsibility of being a father.

Just as her heart began to throb, the bedroom door opened, and in walked the man of her dreams carrying two steamy cups of Burger King coffee and her favorite French toast sticks. The familiar sight put a big smile on her face. Domonique sat up, kissed, and hugged Bomani tightly when he sat beside her on the bed.

"Good morning to you too," he said, placing the food and coffee on the nightstand and then sliding his fingers across her bare breasts. He fondled and kissed her some more before she pulled away.

"Bomani, I'm lovin' this and don't want it to end . . ."

"How come I feel like there's a 'but' following that statement?"

"Because you know me," she answered, looking him in the eyes. "I know I said I wasn't going to ask questions, but that was before you said that you want to claim your place in our daughter's life." Domonique took hold of his hand and held it in both of hers. "Bo, I need you to tell me what's going on. What was last night at that house about?"

Bomani took a deep breath, then handed her a coffee. He took a sip of his own and started explaining everything that had brought him there.

"I invested all of Sen's and my savings with this investment company out in the Chi, and to cut a long story short, I mixed business with pleasure, and it fucked me over in the end."

"So, you got played out of all y'all's money?" she asked, shocked. "Well, I guess it's good y'all were able to get it back," she said, eyeing the money he'd given her.

"Not all of it. What he had there wasn't even close. I know there's nothing I can do to change the past, but damn, I wish..." Bomani shook his head in disappointment with himself. "I was thinking about adding another spot to hit before—"

"No!" she said quickly, cutting him off. "You said y'all were out, especially after how you said doing that shit has changed Sen."

"Yeah, Bae, but I don't see what other choice I got."

"If you need money, I'll be more than happy to give that back to you," she said, pointing toward the dresser. "And if you need more, I have about fifty thousand dollars saved that I'll split with you," Domonique said sincerely.

"Thanks, Babee, but I can't take your money. That's for you and my little princess in there." He gave her a peck on the lips. "But you're right. I'mma just stick to the one that I already got planned out for us, and then we're done."

"I don't think you should do that one either, Bo," she said, pleading with her eyes. "You can call it what you want, but I don't have a good feeling about it."

"I have to go through with it. I told you Shiesty and DB both got fucked up with the law back-to-back, and I promised that I'd look out for them."

Domonique rolled her eyes and let out an animated sigh, making sure he understood that she was getting annoyed with his "Brother's Keeper" way of thinking.

"Bo, you can't keep on bailing those two out every time they mess up. You have a daughter who needs you to look out for her. You just promised us that you'll be here for us. Now you're saying that you're going to risk everything for them *Can't Get Right* friends of yours. Bo, you know I love them, but you also know I'm right."

"Nique, I really need you to be patient with me. You know all they've been through with us. I just can't turn my back on 'em right now. I know neither one of them *'Can't Get Rights'* would turn their back on me or any one of us," Bomani said with conviction. "This one last time, and I'm all yours. I was planning to move outta the Mil afterwards anyway. Now I got down there with you two to make my new home. Man, Nique, motherhood has really changed you. It's a good thing—I like it on you," he smiled. "Will you just let me finish what I started?"

"You know you just left the door open for me to say that I am letting you finish what you started by allowing you here with us. But I'm not going to say it," she smiled back. "You better come back to us!" she threatened after sitting there silent for a moment, giving what he was asking some thought. "And when you do come back, I need you to know that I want the white picket fence and all that."

Domonique's trusty woman's intuition was screaming that she was allowing the man she still very much loved to make a big mistake. Something about it all just didn't feel right. The job Bomani was telling her about sounded forced, and the Bomani she knew didn't move like that. Now that she had him and Sentrice back in her life, nothing else really seemed to matter. The last thing she wanted was for them to get caught or hurt robbing a place just when their lives were beginning to change for the better.

A few hours later, as Domonique and Blessing watched Bomani and Sentrice's plane take off, all she could do was wonder if she'd made the right choice by allowing Bomani into their daughter's life or not. Standing there at the window, she closed her eyes and said a quick prayer for Bomani and Sentrice's safety and one for his safe return.

"Mama, why are you crying?"

"I'm okay, baby, I just hate goodbyes like this," Domonique answered, wiping her eyes, then scooping her daughter up and carrying her back out of the airport.

Chapter 30

The day of the siblings' return, attorney Rosenberg had Shiesty meet him down at the district police station for the meeting he'd set up with the detectives concerning the incident that had taken place inside Shiesty's home. The meeting went just as Rosenberg had promised it would. A pair of detectives interviewed Shiesty with the lawyer in the room. He told the detectives no more than Rosenberg instructed him to, and Shiesty was allowed to walk out a free man with a request that he not skip town anytime soon without giving the detectives notice.

Immediately after leaving the station, Shiesty headed to the airport to pick up his friends, whose plane was due to touch down within the next 45 minutes after his meeting.

***

Jaheim was sitting in a parking lot across the street from the police precinct after picking up a few items from the store for his aunt. That's when he spotted Detective Hermon walking someone out the rear of the station with a tight grip on his arm, but no handcuffs. This fact made Jaheim believe that the man was one of the punk detective's confidential informants. The pure thug shook his head at the snitch, but his curiosity made him keep watching the scene.

Jaheim observed Hermon briskly walk the man to the rear of what looked to be a delivery van and help him inside.

Since Jaheim had a rocky history with the detective, he waited until the phony delivery van drove off before pulling out of the parking lot and going in the opposite direction. It was in that direction that he was able to see the man who had gotten away from him being escorted into the precinct by a short man in a fancy blue suit that screamed *lawyer*. Jaheim's first thought was to park, wait until the guy came back out, and follow him, but he kept going because he knew Chief Ken was satisfied with whoever he had collected vengeance on for the murder of his kids' mother.

***

When Sentrice made it back to Milwaukee, the first thing she did was text her man. She asked Jaheim to meet her at her house so he could show her how much he missed her. As soon as she sent the text, Bomani informed her and Shiesty that he was calling a meeting and for them to meet him at their clubhouse in two hours.

Sentrice was vexed by her brother's timing, but she knew that him finding out about his daughter had put a lot on his mind and assumed that the sudden meeting was about him now moving to Florida instead of Georgia. On the plane ride back, all he could talk about was Blessing. Sentrice was a little jealous of her brother's happiness but happy for him at the same time.

"Hey, let's have a little get-together?" Sentrice suggested.

"That's not a bad idea. We can do it at my crib, and you can bring that mystery nigga of yours over so I can see what's to him."

"So *we* can see what's to him," Shiesty corrected with a slight growl to his voice.

"Boy, y'all ain't scaring nobody. He'll be there," she promised.

Sentrice wondered what her and Jaheim's child would look like and if he would be as proud as Bomani if she were to get pregnant.

When Shiesty pulled up in front of her brother's place, she slid out of the backseat and headed straight to her car.

"Sen, I'm serious about the meeting!" Bomani yelled behind her. "We gon' have it right after the lil get-together."

"I know, I know, I won't be that late!" she retorted as she quickly got in her car and smashed off, laughing at her brother's facial expression because of what she'd said.

After almost two hours of mind-blowing sex, Sentrice and Jaheim were rejuvenated as they pulled up in Jaheim's freshly waxed car in front of Bomani's house. Sentrice looked over at her big brother's house, then over at her date, and started to feel like butterflies were playing tag in her stomach. She was more nervous than she thought she'd be about Jaheim meeting Bomani and the guys. She suspected that her overprotective friends were probably going to try to be intimidating, and she didn't want Jaheim to feel uncomfortable. Then she looked at him and knew that Jaheim wouldn't be easily intimidated like the others before him.

"Hey, you, is there a reason we're just sittin' here?"

"No, baby, I'm just a little nervous all of a sudden," Sentrice confessed.

"That's understandable, but you gotta stop being nervous because you're starting to make me feel some kinda way. Hey, I can go park somewhere ducked off and help you relax real quick?" Jaheim said, grinning as he ran his fingers up and down her thigh.

"Ummm, Jah, stop it." She playfully brushed his hand away. "I feel like I'ma need all of that and more later, but right now, let's go on up in there."

Sentrice checked her face in the mirror, then stepped out of the car. Holding hands, she led Jaheim up to the front door.

As soon as the happy couple stepped foot inside the house, they saw a small crowd that looked to be having a good time drinking and smoking a citrus-smelling kush that made Jaheim's mouth water.

Kevin Gates' and Internet Money's song "No Option" boomed through the surround sound speakers:

"There was no shoes that I walk in, Had to make it out, I had no option . . ."

Jaheim looked around and saw a couple of girls that he knew from *The Gentlemen's Club* and prayed that Sentrice wasn't the crazy jealous type. Sentrice saw the expression on his face and felt like they both could use a drink before anything. She led him over to the bar table, where they helped themselves to a drink.

Jaheim took a swallow of his vodka and cranberry and was about to give Sentrice a heads-up on the girls he knew there when he spotted another face that he'd never thought he would see mingling across the room.

"What the fuck, really?" he said more to himself than to Sentrice as he turned away, trying not to be seen and wishing he could avoid the man—or better yet, that the man wouldn't recognize him without his mask.

"Hey, Shiesty, I want you to meet somebody," Sentrice said after waving her friend over to the bar. Then she spun Jaheim back around. "Shiesty, meet my man Jah. Jah, this isn't my brother, but he likes to act like one to me," she said, introducing the two.

"I've been waiting to meet you, Jah," Shiesty said, not recognizing the man who had tried to kill him just days ago. He gave Jaheim a fist bump. "Sen, since you're introducing me to your guy, let me introduce you to my friend Tamara," Shiesty said.

Chapter 31

Jaheim found the guy who was holding the kush he'd been craving since he walked through the door and bought a blunt of it. Then he stood around smoking, sipping, and enjoying the view of a couple of girls twerking to the song *Body* by Megan Thee Stallion. When the show was over, he glanced at his watch and saw that Sentrice had been gone for over fifteen minutes. He wondered if everything was alright with her and her brother. Jaheim also wondered if they were discussing him since Sentrice had been so nervous about the two of them meeting.

Earlier, while waiting for Sentrice to make introductions, Jaheim was unknowingly spotted by a female friend of Mia's. Mia was a woman Jaheim used to hook up with from time to time before he met Sentrice. On sight of seeing Jaheim at the party, all cozy with Sentrice, the instigator promptly snapped a couple of shots of the two together and sent them to her friend.

Approximately twenty minutes later, a jealous, angry Mia arrived, making her way through the crowd to where Jaheim stood, locked in a conversation with some guys he had just met about criminal justice reform and systemic racism.

"I feel you on that. The big homie is sitting up north doing a 40- or 50-year sentence on an imperfect self-defense charge right now. Meanwhile, they got this lil white kid who came up to Kenosha with his racist-ass buddies, shooting niggas at random, back home in Illinois living it up," Jaheim said, referring to an incident that happened during the riots after the police shooting of Jacob Blake.

"Yeah, you talkin' 'bout that Carl Whiter-House or whatever that kid name is. Ya know, his ass was on video or some shit talkin' about how he was going up to Wisconsin for some real target practice. All they asses should be locked the fuck up—his fool-ass mother, the muthafucka who gave him the gun, and them ones that brought him there to do that shit," one of the guys replied.

"I'm all the way with you on that, but from the way it's looking, they gon' let him off with a slap on the wrist. I'm no lawyer, but everything about what he did screams intentional homicide. Where, in my homie's case, he protected himself against a person that had been threatening him and damaging his property for months. Even at the time of the shooting, his victim had been following him and threatening him. Wisconsin's self-defense law states:

1. That retreat is not an option, meaning you don't have to run from a muthafucka if you don't want to.
2. That we're allowed to protect ourselves, our property, and others from real or perceived danger using the force necessary to stop the threat.

So, in the dark, my homie mistook a cellphone for the gun that had been pulled on him in the past and shot first. Yeah, I brought the case up because it's personal to me, but it's a lot of cases like it. Remember the George Webb shooting, where the guy tried to hit them females with a coffee pot filled with hot coffee, and one of their guys shot him to stop the threat? That dude got like 30 years for that."

"I'll say it if you won't. It's because they're Black, that's it, that's all. You remember that Zimmerman punk down south that followed and killed that lil unarmed Martin kid? They let him off because he's white and killed a Black boy. So yeah, all this shit needs to change."

"Excuse me," Mia said, stepping up behind Jaheim. "Jaheim, come talk to me," she whispered in his ear. She gave him no reason to think she was on anything.

"Mia? Whud up?" Jaheim asked, a bit shocked to see her there.

Mia led him over by the kitchen, where it was a little easier to talk over the music of the party going on around them. There, she went in on him about blowing her off for Sentrice.

"So, you can be all out here partying with the next bitch, making me look like a fool to my friends cuz I'm sitting around waiting on you and shit?" she snapped, waving her phone with one of the photos of him and Sentrice together on its screen in his face. "What is this bitch's pussy made of, gold or something? Because she ain't as fine as me with her big-head ass!"

"I ain't makin' you look like a damn thing. You're doing that on your own. Mia, you knew what it was with us from the jump. We had fun, and now it's over. So get yo' drunk ass outta my face!"

"Or what, Jah? What? You gon' beat my ass?" Mia exclaimed, getting in his face, putting on more of a scene while trying to provoke him into a fight with her.

"Bitch, I ain't 'bout to do this with you! You can stand yo' silly ass here and fight with yo' damn self!" he growled at her, then out of habit put on his mask as he turned his back on her to walk away. That's when he saw Shiesty charging straight for him.

On the other side of the room, Shiesty had been observing what was going on between Sentrice's new boyfriend and a female he'd never seen before. Shiesty had just sent Sentrice and Bomani a text telling them to come see what was going on. When he looked up from his phone, Jaheim had turned, facing him with his mask on. It was like a light switch had flipped on—Shiesty recognized him as one of the men who had run up in his house.

"Bitch-ass nigga, you tried to come for me like it was sweet!" Shiesty yelled, his face contorted in rage as he simultaneously swung a half-full bottle of champagne at Jaheim's head.

Jaheim jerked away from Mia's pleading grip and, with no hesitation, moving lightning quick like a top light-heavyweight MMA fighter, Jaheim easily dodged the lumbering strike from his enraged adversary. Instantly, Jaheim threw his right arm against his head and blocked Shiesty's wild swing at his dome. He immediately ducked under Shiesty's arm, slipped behind him, and shoved him away.

Chapter 32

Shiesty was slow to get his wits back in order, but when he did, the first thing he did was scan the crowd for the face of the man who'd knocked him out. Shiesty kept screaming, asking, "Where is he?" as he walked—still wobbly—around in circles.

"He's gone. Fam, you need to sit down before you fall down," DB said, following behind him like a concerned parent teaching a baby to walk.

"C'mere, I need to holla at you for a second!" Shiesty said, roughly grabbing Sentrice by the arm and half-dragging her into her brother's bedroom.

Bomani followed them inside, leaving DB to tend to the guests and the mess that was made of his home. Bomani closed the door behind the three of them to keep the inquisitives from putting more of his family's business out in the streets or on social media.

"What da fuck do you think you finna do to my sister, Shiesty? Nigga, check yo'self and let her go!" Bomani demanded, knocking Shiesty's hand off her.

"Bo, I ain't on that with her, even though she brought the nigga here!" Shiesty glared, fuming at Sentrice. "My head's bleedin' and shit! She always doing dumb shit!" he exclaimed, feeling around the area of the gash high on his temple.

"Bitch, you the one dumb! From what I heard, you the one who ran up on him, and Jah tapped that ass. I'm sick and tired of this shit! You ain't my brother and never will be, with yo' ole jealous ass."

"Sen, chill!" Bomani barked. "Here, hold this on yo' head to try and slow up some of that bleeding. Shiesty, say what you gotta say while I look for my lil first-aid kit," Bomani said, tossing him a clean white T-shirt. He then went rummaging through the closet looking for the kit.

"Nawl, not this time, Bo. This nigga think just 'cause I let him nibble on this pussy one time on some ole drunk shit that he can fuckin' keep getting in my business! But you see I got the right nigga for that ass this time," Sentrice snapped, walking toward the door. "Jah is my man. I love him, and I'll never be with you! And Bo, I don't care whether you like Jah or if you don't like him. I'm grown, and I don't need your approval on who I love! I love him, and he loves me, and that's all that matters since you wanna take sides!" she said, her hand resting on the doorknob.

"I ain't takin' shit! I'm just tryna find out what happened between them two niggas. Now I know," Bomani retorted, staring down Shiesty for having sex with his sister behind his back.

"Bo, it ain't even like that. She don't know what she talkin' about."

"So she lying about y'all fuckin' around behind my back?"

"No, I'm not saying that, and that wasn't supposed to happen, I know. But like she said, we were both on some drunk shit. And I ain't ever came at her again. What happened here ain't about her. That's one of the niggas that ran up in my crib and killed Mam-man and my lil bitch," Shiesty told them.

A look of total disbelief covered Sentrice's face. It took a hot moment for her to fully process what Shiesty had just told them. She immediately began feeling like someone was squeezing her heart. Everything about the way Jaheim is around her was so right. She couldn't see him as a grimey-ass dude that'd be on that type of time. But then she remembered that that was also the same day Jaheim came in talking about how he got jumped. She shook the negative thoughts off, trying to convince herself that Shiesty was lying about her perfect man being the wrong man for her.

"Shiesty, are you sure Jah was one of 'em? You said they had on masks, so it could've been just some dude that looks like him."

"Sen, it was him," he told her. "I didn't know at first but felt some kinda way when you introduced us, like I knew him from somewhere. And yeah, I was kinda on that, but it's him." Shiesty confessed to feeling a little jealous. "But when I seen him talkin' to ole girl with his mask on, there was no question if he was one of 'em or not. I can't forget a nigga that tried to kill me!"

"So you're saying Jah knew who you was from the start and didn't say or do shit until I was gone?"

"That's what it seems like to me."

"Sen, you didn't tell him about what we do? Or has he been askin' a bunch of questions about who I am or who you hang around with?" Bomani asked, the wheels turning in his head about why Jaheim was really around his sister.

"No, he never asked me anything. I know better than to talk about what we do to anybody that's not one of us," she answered without hesitation, assuring them that she wasn't lying.

"Fam, tell me one more time how that shit went down at yo' crib, and don't leave nothin' out," Bomani instructed. Then he stood there with his arms crossed, listening to every word Shiesty said he remembered from the night at his house.

"I think that boy workin' for somebody we hit, since you sayin' that he was more focused on who we are than the bread you offered him to leave."

"Yeah, so he might be using yo' silly ass to get to us, Sen, and you just let him in our business!" Shiesty said to her, half-wincing from the pain of his head wound.

"Fuck you, Shiesty! I said I ain't tell him shit, and I didn't!" she retorted, ready to fight him herself now.

"Y'all two chill the fuck out!" Bomani said. "Fam, go out there and have folks take you to go get stitched up. I'ma finish hollering at Sis and see what's to ole boy. And tell everybody the party's over out there."

"Bo, I'm good. She just need to tell us where that nigga live at."

"You ain't good, my nigga. Now go get fixed up so I can holla at Sentrice," Bomani instructed.

Shiesty wanted to protest but knew he wouldn't get anywhere with Bomani if he did. So he did as he was told. Once the siblings were alone, Bomani really pressed his sister for more information about her new boyfriend.

"Bo, I was right there looking both of them in they faces when I introduced them. Shiesty might be wrong about Jah."

"Sen, it's hard for me to believe that. How long have we been dealing with fam? You know how he is with faces."

"Yeah, if it's a bitch. He don't pay niggas no mind."

"What's his address? I'ma go holla at him myself and see what's to him," Bomani said as he retrieved his gun from beneath his mattress.

"I don't know it, and I don't remember how to get there. Jaheim lives in Sussex. I only been to his place twice at night. You know I like to be in my own bed."

"Please tell me, how are you so in love with a muthafucka you don't know shit about?" Bomani chastised. Sentrice couldn't do anything but just stand there, feeling embarrassed. "This shit right here is why I stand on you the way I do, Sen. It's not about me controlling you. I'm the way I am over you because I don't want to see you get used or hurt," Bomani said in a softer tone of voice.

Sentrice knew that she had a choice to make. Her options were to break up with Jaheim—where in that choice, she would have to kill him—or to choose love and run away with him, because she felt in her heart that what they have is real. As she struggled with it on the inside, on the outside a wave of tears streamed from her eyes.

"Bo, I love him," she sobbed.

Hating to see her cry, Bomani quickly pulled her to him and held his sister close.

"I know you do, but it's not real. If Shiesty's memory is right, then . . . I'ma let you handle this, because regardless of how we feel, we can't feel what you're feeling. You know him the way you do, so Sen, you handle it. Now go in there and fix your face before you go see him. You don't need to let him see that you've been crying."

Once the house was cleared, Shiesty refused to be taken to the hospital, so Bomani ordered Sentrice to patch him up the best she could. While she worked on closing the inch-long gash on Shiesty's head, the incident between him and Jaheim—laced with the possibility that Jaheim might be working for the cartel, or one of the people they'd robbed who works for the cartel—had Bomani's thoughts racing. Domonique's pleas for him to call everything off kept repeating in his head, but he knew that he needed the money for them all to be straight before he ran off to keep his promise to his girl and child. The only choice for Bomani was to get money, so he called the meeting right then and there.

"What's going on that we're having this meeting now?" DB inquired without stopping his cleaning. He needed to keep himself busy to hide his nervousness due to the wire he was carrying in his pocket.

"Well, because of all of this new weird BS that's going around, I've made my mind up to get the fuck outta dodge sooner than I'd planned on leaving."

"So what I'm hearing is that you're calling off the lick that you had planned for us?" DB spoke with a clear attitude. "So, since y'all went and got some of y'all's bread back, it's back to fuck the rest of us again?"

"DB, what's up with you lately? I told you that I got you, and for your info: I gave Rosy most of that lil change that I had. So I need some paper just like you do. Which is why we gonna hit 'em tomorrow," Bomani said, dropping into his favorite chair.

"I thought you said they do the big pickup on Thursdays. What changed?" DB questioned, not because he really cared to know but because he wanted to make sure the detectives listening got what they needed.

"Everything, but don't trip—it'll be enough for us to live good for a minute or longer if y'all check y'all spending," Bomani answered.

Sentrice's heart was hurting, and her head wasn't right to be doing anything, but if her brother was going to do it tomorrow, then so was she.

"Bro, whatever you say, I'm in. Let me use one of your cars so I can go and clean up my mess," she said, excusing herself and leaving.

Chapter 33

When Sentrice made it back to her place, she immediately noticed that Jaheim's car was nowhere to be found, telling her he wasn't waiting inside for her. She entered her home into soft lighting and the intoxicating sound of Avant passionately singing his song, *When It Hurts*, on the radio. Sentrice knew that Jaheim had been there and gone because the radio wasn't on before they left to go to her brother's house. She made her way straight over to the bar, poured herself a heavy glass of Patrón with a touch of lemon, and then sat down on the sofa. Sipping on her drink and wondering where Jaheim was and why he wasn't calling her back, she began looking around the room for her house key. Seeing that he had left it made her relax some and focus on the words of the song that he'd left on repeat:

"I'ma need your undivided attention / 'Cause it's fantasies and reality / Baby, which one are we livin' in? Oh / When it hurts, will we still be / The same two lovers all over each other, will we? / When it hurts, will we still see / Why we got together . . ."

Sitting and listening to the song, she couldn't believe that the man who once made her look like a shy school girl was now a suspect in a web of deceit.

***

133

"I don't know if you're tryna play me for a fool or not, so I'ma ask you this, and I want a truthful answer."

"Wow, so now you think I've been lying to you about shit? Wow!"

"Bae, I don't know what to think right about now. But I need to know—have you had any run-ins with Shiesty before today?" she asked, waving at LaQuess, who had waved at her from the stage.

Jaheim looked her in the eyes for the first time since she'd sat next to him. Then, he looked into his glass and downed his drink, raking his brain for the right response.

"Sen, before we get into all of that, I think we should go back to your crib to have this conversation."

"Okay . . . okay, I think so too. Just let me enjoy a drink or two first," she nervously agreed and began taking tiny sips of her Patrón, trying to think of significant ways to make her time with him last before the crashing end she felt looming in their future. "On second thought, let's just go now, 'cause I'ma need more than a drink or two for what I believe you're about to tell me."

After finishing her drink, they walked outside together. Alone in her vehicle, Sentrice couldn't keep her eyes off her rearview mirror. She was leading the way back to her place when, all of a sudden, she started feeling apprehensive about being alone with the man of her dreams. At her home, she released her inner seductress, swaying her hips in a way that was sure to turn Jaheim on and keep his eyes on her behind and his tipsy mind off the reason they were there. Unlocking the door, she remembered that she'd left her gun in the car, so as soon as they stepped inside, Sentrice pushed him against the door, wrapping her arms around him in a feverish kiss that Jaheim eagerly returned. Then, just as suddenly as the kiss had started, it abruptly ended with her snatching his gun off his waist and turning it on him.

"So this is what it's come down to between us?" he asked with pure hurt in his eyes.

"This is what it really was from the start with you. How long have you known about me?"

"I've known about you . . . and your guys for a while. But I didn't find out about your involvement until tonight at the party—and I still wasn't sure then," he told her honestly.

"If that's so, why didn't you tell me what you do from the jump?" she asked, fighting the tears burning her eyes.

"How do you tell somebody something like that? You can answer your own question, 'cause you didn't tell me that you rob niggas for a living," Jaheim said. "Listen to me, baby. The contract that was out on y'all has been called off. It was way before today. I swear to you that I didn't know anything about you being a part of the crew I'd been looking for before now. But it's over. Baby, we—"

"Your bullshit ruined our whole relationship! So you damn right it's over!" Sentrice snapped, cutting him off as tears ran down her face.

"No, wait, Sentrice . . . I think your boy DB is an informant," Jaheim blurted. He knew he shouldn't have told her this without proof, but he was trying to do everything in his power to persuade Sentrice not to break up with him.

"What?"

"I seen him talking to this punk-ass detective twice now. Once this morning down on 3rd Street, and again when I was leaving your brother's house. I don't know what he's doing with him, but if he's talking to him in any way, I'm betting the punk might know all about the robberies y'all did and everything he needs to build a case," he explained. "Please, baby, believe me when I tell you I love you!" Jaheim inched his way toward her.

"Stop! Don't come any closer!" Sentrice shouted, aiming the gun at Jaheim's belly.

He ignored her threat and kept coming until he was close enough to grab the gun. Cautiously, he took hold of it and gently removed it from her loose grip. Empty-handed, Sentrice immediately swung on him, hitting him in his chest, shoulders, and wherever the emotional confusion she was experiencing directed her fists.

"Baby, stop it. Stop! Sen, I'm not going to fight with you," Jaheim said, pulling Sentrice close and hugging her tight as she cried her eyes out. "I can never do anything to intentionally hurt you," he swore, placing tender kisses all over her face. When his lips reached hers, she fought to resist kissing him back—and lost.

Jaheim tossed the gun aside into a chair and pushed her down onto the sofa. Sentrice held onto his shirt, taking him down with her. The two of them bounced and rolled onto the floor, landing between the sofa and coffee table.

"Ja!"

"I love you!" he confessed as he unfastened her pants.

Sentrice said nothing in retort. She just gave in to the warmth of his hands against her skin as he slipped his fingers into her jeans and panties, dragging them off over her hips. Fortuitously, her thighs parted, revealing her swollen blossom to him. Sentrice continued to pound on his shoulders with her fists even after Jaheim began slowly running his tongue down her inner thigh until it was in her wetness, exploring her silky crevices. Jaheim kissed, licked, and sucked on her blossom, knowing it could be the last time. Sentrice never wanted the moment to end as the first of her orgasms took over her body, causing her legs to tremble. She locked her ankles together behind his head and rolled her hips, feeding herself to him. Jaheim broke free, sliding up over her until she felt his hardness parting her. He drove it further and further inside her tight walls.

"Oh, oooh, oh, shhhhiiit, you in my stomach!" she exclaimed, spreading her legs even wider.

He started out with slow, deep, deliberate strokes, then turned into a beast when she clawed his neck, shoulder, and forearm. Sentrice's moans grew louder and louder with each hard plunge he delivered until she felt him exploding, filling her with his essence.

Jaheim collapsed on top of her, and she held him tightly well after her climax. For the next ten minutes or so, the two just laid there in silence, listening to each other's heartbeats as Avant continued to sing them to sleep:

"When it hurts, will we still be / The same two lovers all over each other? / When it hurts . . ."

Hours later, but still early morning, Jaheim got up and got dressed. He grabbed his gun from the chair and whispered that he loved her before walking out the door.

"I love you too," Sentrice whispered, thinking she was hearing him in her dream until she reached over and found that he was gone. She quickly got up and dashed to the window just as Jaheim's Hellcat pulled off. She walked back over to the sofa and noticed a little black ring box sitting on top of a pink napkin from the club, lying on the pillow where Jaheim's head had been moments ago.

"Oh no, no, no, nooo!" she squealed aloud. Her hands trembled as she picked it up and opened it. Inside, she found a beautiful, clear, deep blue sapphire and white diamond ring. She blinked away tears as she read the handwritten note that accompanied it.

Chapter 34

Detective Lont watched her overeager temporary partner, Hermon, as he pulled up the GPS map of the area of the murderous robbery crew's next hit—good information that they had collected off the wire their CI had on him during the meeting with his crew. From the look on her face, it was clear that she had issues with Hermon's rushed plan to take the crew down, but there was nothing she could do about it now because he'd gone behind her back to the captain with the information and gotten the green light on the arrest warrants.

"As we all know from their past robberies, the leader of this crew is a crafty son-of-a-bitch," Hermon said, addressing the small group of officers assigned to assist with the arrests. "We've learned that he plans to skip town after their next job and that the date of that job has been moved up to tomorrow afternoon. I do not believe the change of plans has anything to do with him knowing that we're on to them, so we still have the element of surprise on our side. But that doesn't mean you shouldn't have your guards up with these guys. They are killers who will not hesitate to kill a cop or anyone else that gets in their way."

"If any one of you happens to get one of them cornered, wait for backup. I repeat, wait for backup. Do not engage them alone, and if you do not have any other option, don't hesitate to use deadly force."

***

"Who else here? 'Cause what we need to talk about don't nobody else need to hear?" Sentrice asked, looking past him into his bedroom.

"Ain't nobody else here, whuddup?" he answered, turning around and going back to get dressed.

"Bo, DB is an informant."

"Informant? Sis, you're trippin'." He huffed. "It ain't no way fam ever gon' be on no shit like that. We've been knowing him since forever, so who's he tellin' on?"

"He's a snitch. DB is working with the police... to get us!"

"That's crazy! Where you hear that from?" Bomani asked, now dressed in jeans and pulling on a plain ash-gray t-shirt.

"Jaheim told me."

"Jaheim?" Bomani snapped. "That fuck-boy's word means what to me? Girl, he got you trippin' like a muthafucka, fuckin' up yo' judgment and shit!"

"I'm straight! My judgment ain't fucked up. I know Jah loves me and wouldn't lie to me about this," Sentrice said defensively. "Plus, why would he lie about DB when he into it with Shiesty?"

"To make you do this dumb shit right here. It's called divide and conquer, one of the oldest tricks in the world!" Bomani shouted with a disgusted look on his face.

"Bo, Jah knows about the detective that DB is talkin' to," she said with an attitude. She had a feeling that her brother wouldn't believe her when she told him who told her about DB. "And you said it yo'self last night that the nigga been acting funny lately," she reminded him.

Bomani sat there thinking. She was right. He *had* noticed that DB had been acting strange lately, pressing him for dates and times on top of vanishing for hours at a time. Like his old mentor used to say: If it smells like a rat, treat it like a rat, because it's better to be safe than sorry.

"You trust this nigga that much?" He watched her slowly nod her head yes. "I can't afford to call this off. You know I gotta be right for my girls when I go back down there."

"I know, and neither can I," Sentrice agreed.

"But you know we're gonna need all four of us to pull this off," Bomani said, sitting on the bed in thought.

"We can use DB for the job and then deal with him afterwards. I'll kill his rat ass if you can't do it."

"I can't see my nigga being a snitch."

"I don't wanna believe it either, but trust me," she said seriously.

"I do, and I'll handle DB, 'cause he has to go, and I need to know why," Bomani said. "Sen, I'm sorry that your guy turned out to be on the other side. I can tell that you really care for him. Ain't no nigga ever had you ready to go to blows with me over him."

"It wasn't even like that." She looked into her brother's eyes and knew that his words were sincere. "Bo, if you really mean that, then . . . you'll be happy if I choose my happiness," she said, carefully removing the napkin from her pocket and handing it to him to read.

"What's this?"

"Just read it."

1 sunny dayMaybe 2 dayz b4 SundayWe had our first play dayMy first perfect dayIt lasted from then 'til Sunday

But each and every day sinceMy life has made no senseHoldin' U in my arms U make me feelTight in your arms this feeling can't be realI've never met another like UIt's true, I've never known a lover to be trueUntil the day U took me thereU made me careOnly U have my heart racing, fighting for airTearfully lying beside UStaring at twinklin' stars wishin' 4 a new day,Fresh air and new lifeAll is possible if you say yes to bein' my wife?

"Is this real?" Bo asked after reading the note.

"Yeah," she answered sadly, showing him the ring box. "It was waiting for me when I woke up this morning."

"Damn . . ." Bomani said, handing her back the note and dropping his head in thought. He had to really think to map out everything perfectly, because all it took was one mistake for him and his sister to end up dead. Life in a cage was not an option for either of them.

"What you over there thinking about?" she asked, sitting down beside him.

"I think we should take the transporters tonight on their way out, like I'd planned at first. And we don't tell the others until it's close to go time."

"So we catch everybody off guard." Sentrice smiled. "Sounds like a plan to me."

"Then that's what we're gonna do. Now, sis, get the fuck outta my crib and go lockdown your happiness before I come to my senses," he told her with a proud smile.

Chapter 35

On 35th Street, right off the highway, Jaheim sat parked in a lonely gas station lot, waiting for the transporters to pull up. In exchange for the nice discount on the product he'd purchased, Chief Ken had also asked Jaheim to escort the cartel's collectors during their cash pickups. At the time, Jaheim had happily agreed, but that was the day before all hell broke loose in his life. Now, he was trying to focus on his task, but the only thing on his mind was Sentrice. He wasn't ready to give her up. Jaheim had told himself, when he reluctantly left her sleeping, that as long as he kept moving, he'd be alright. But even after a long, hot shower, he could still taste her on his lips. He knew her taste was all in his head, but the pain their breakup left in his heart was real. Sentrice was everything he wanted, and he wanted to give her his all by making her his forever.

Jaheim had been looking forward to proposing to her after winning her brother's approval that day because he knew Bomani's approval meant something to her. Sentrice's happiness was all that mattered to him. He wondered if she would've said yes when he asked her to marry him. With that thought, he went to look at her photo on his cellphone and realized he didn't have it with him. As he thought about where it could be, he didn't remember having it when he got in his house that morning. He smiled and chuckled to himself because he knew he'd left it at her place.

Jaheim received a text, snapping him out of his thoughts of Sentrice. He saw it was from the transporters informing him that they were at the meeting spot. He looked around and spotted two Cadillac SUVs turning onto the gas station's lot.

Jaheim instantly knew this was who he was waiting for, so he flashed his lights, then sent them a text letting them know it was him. They texted back, telling him to leave his car and ride with them. Obediently, he put the phone away, grabbed his gun, and got out of his car. The driver of the truck closest to him got out and moved to the backseat, leaving the door ajar. Jaheim knew what that meant. He climbed into the driver's seat of the lead truck and immediately headed off toward the first of the drop-and-pickup locations.

***

Sentrice sat in the driver's seat of a stolen dark gray BMW, her hands gripping the steering wheel like it was meant to keep her in place. Beside her sat Shiesty, staring down the block. They were parked a block and a half away from the car wash where the collectors were supposed to make their last pickup before heading back out of the city.

"Heads up, here they come," Shiesty announced.

Sentrice didn't respond. Her mind was stuck on her possible engagement to Jaheim. All kinds of thoughts about a wedding, children, and a future with her man filled her head when she needed to be focused on the job.

"Where are you?" she mumbled to herself.

"Sen? Sen? Are you with me?" Shiesty asked, snapping his fingers to get her attention. "I said, here they come. Call Bo, because he didn't say shit about it being two of 'em."

She turned to Shiesty with an annoyed look.

"You still trippin' after all that happened? Are we alright?"

"Yeah, I'm good and we're good. Let's do this so I can get on with my life," Sentrice said, rolling her eyes and pulling up a mask with sexy red vampire lips on it. She picked up her gun from between her legs and made sure it was ready for action. "It's okay. We're gonna hit the one in the back—it's where the money's at. Bo got word on it a lil' before we headed out. That's why the times and shit changed. He just forgot to tell you." She lied.

***

Two blocks on the other side of the car wash, DB sat behind the wheel of the stolen Audi, trying his best to keep a calm expression on his face. He knew how important this day was—it was a step closer to his new freedom. Over in the passenger seat sat Bomani. He was deathly quiet, with a no-nonsense expression on his face and his M4 resting in his lap. The only thing on his mind was completing the mission at hand, especially since he had a deal with DB right afterwards.

Being broke wasn't an option now that he knew about his little girl. This last mission would set him straight financially, allowing him to live off the money from the heist while getting to better know his daughter.

"Here we go," Bomani said as he watched twin charcoal-gray Cadillac Escalades pull up to the back of the car wash.

Bomani quickly pulled up his mask and held his weapon in a firm grip. His entire future depended on this one job. He watched as two men stepped out of the front SUV and entered the building.

"Let's go!" DB quickly stomped down on the accelerator, and the Audi took off. Once the car was close enough, DB tapped the brake and yanked the wheel, causing the Audi to slide and stop helter-skelter in front of the SUVs. Seconds later, the BMW did the exact same maneuver behind the back SUV, boxing them in.

Bomani quickly hopped out of the car and aimed his M4 at the driver. He immediately saw the driver pick up his gun. In a regular situation, Bomani would've shot the driver instantly, but today, he knew the meaning of the eyes staring back at him from behind the windshield. So instead, he fired a three-round burst into the empty passenger seat as a warning.

"Hands up!" he ordered Jaheim while shaking his head silently, telling him not to test him if he wanted to live.

Chapter 36

Behind the truck, Shiesty jumped out of the passenger seat of the BMW and headed straight for the back door of the second Cadillac truck. He didn't bother with words or opening the doors; he just heartlessly sprayed hot lead through the windows and doors, hitting everyone inside. Once he saw that there was no more movement from the men, Shiesty snatched open the back of the truck and began grabbing bags of money, running them back to the BMW. Shiesty climbed out of the back of the truck for the third time just as two armed men came running out of the building. But before they had a chance to do anything, Bomani appeared from in front of the lead truck, quickly gunning them both down. Shiesty returned the favor by covering Bomani's back while he ran over and collected the bags of money that one of the men was carrying.

Exchanging salutes, both of them turned and dashed to their getaway cars. Bomani looked back and saw Shiesty jump in the BMW with the money. Instantly, the car peeled off like a rocket, heading in the opposite direction just as planned. Smiling behind his mask, Bomani fired once more through the windshield of the truck Jaheim was in, then ran and hopped in the Audi.

"Go, go, go!" he yelled, tossing the bags in the back seat.

DB stomped down on the accelerator, and the car promptly responded with a roar as its tires squealed, sailing them away from the scene of the crime.

***

Detective Hermon was fuming because things didn't go as he'd planned for the bust. Relentless, he didn't completely call it off. Instead, he ordered everyone to stay in the perimeter of the robbery suspects' targeted area. He was two blocks away when dispatch called in a report of multiple gunshots being fired behind a carwash in his area. Even though dispatch didn't say it, Hermon had a strong gut feeling that the call was about the crew he'd planned to take down that day.

Dispatch reported that the alleged gunmen fled the scene in two cars: one a black BMW and the other a dark gray Audi, both fitting the description of the vehicles Hermon had given DB from the police impound to use in the robbery. Hermon was just about to make a right at the corner when, out of nowhere, a black BMW zoomed past him.

"Hell yeah! Here we go!" he said excitedly to the officer in the passenger seat beside him, who promptly called in that they were in pursuit of the BMW.

The eager detective hastily made a hard U-turn and fell in line directly behind the fleeing car. Hermon didn't want to cause any accidents due to the high-speed chase through the city streets, so he thought he'd outsmart them by slowing down and staying a few cars behind the BMW. When the car slowed, Hermon's first thought was that his unmarked police car didn't look like a police vehicle, so if he stayed cool, he could follow the BMW and let it lead him to the rest of the crew.

The detectives noticed the car stop for a red light. Curious to see the faces of its occupants, Hermon nonchalantly pulled right up beside the car. Glancing over, he saw that the tints on the windows were too dark for him to see through.

When the light turned green, the BMW's driver's window lowered, and the detective saw the sexy lips of the vampire

147

mask and the driver's cold eyes staring back at him. Suddenly, the driver's arm raised, holding a gun, and quickly fired multiple shots. The last thing the officer in the passenger seat saw were the fleeing taillights of the BMW through the blood-splattered windshield, and Hermon's brains all over him, before he passed out.

***

DB floored the Audi, sending them zipping out of the area. He kept his eyes more on his rearview mirror than the road. He was looking for the detectives. He didn't know for sure, but Bomani's sudden change in plans made him more paranoid than he already was about setting up his friends to save himself.

"Fuck! Here come the police!" DB announced, feeling a bit of relief.

"Where da fuck did that car come from?" Bomani exclaimed, turning in his seat to look out the back window. "Try to lose 'em!"

"No shit, Bo!" DB retorted as he weaved from lane to lane in his phony attempt to shake the police cars chasing them.

The Audi's engine growled as it raced through traffic. DB tapped the brake and snatched the wheel, forcing a sharp turn into a narrow alleyway, then repeated the maneuver when the alley came to an end, sending them blazing back into traffic. The unmarked police car, with two MPD squad cars right behind it, skidded helter-skelter but stayed on their tail. DB was impressed that the detective's car didn't crash like one of the police cars did behind it.

Bomani knew that more police were on the way and that they would set up roadblocks to try to stop them. He guessed that DB was taking him right to them, so he had to think fast. Still looking over his shoulder, Bomani watched the police cars zooming through the intersection, avoiding collisions by inches.

"These muthafuckas still behind us!"

"I'm trying to lose 'em," DB said, looking down at the speedometer, which read 98 mph, and easing off the accelerator. Then he whipped the car around a corner, knowing it would stall out from the sudden turn.

"Shit, something's wrong with the car."

"What the fuck! We gonna have to split up," Bomani said, slamming a fresh magazine into the M4.

"No, wait, I got it!" DB said, starting the car back up and pulling off again once he saw Detective Lont catching up to them.

"Fuck this, I can't trust this piece of shit. We're splitting up. The Greyhound station is like three or four blocks from here. Let me out at the corner, then keep going," Bomani said, reaching into the backseat and grabbing one of the bags of money. "Fam, it's only one of them on us now, so he can only go after one of us. Nine times out of ten, they're gonna keep chasing you because of the car," Bomani explained, studying DB's face. "But if, for some crazy reason, they come after me, then I want you to grab that bag, ditch the car as soon as possible, and make your way to yo' crib."

"Why my crib?"

"It's closer for me to get to," Bomani answered, pointing out the obvious.

"I'll meet you there," DB promised seconds before he brought the car to a skidding stop in the middle of traffic, giving Bomani a straight shot to the Greyhound station and the detective a clear view of which way he went.

"You know the rules. Don't get caught!" Bomani instructed. "See you at yo' crib."

"I'll be there," DB replied to Bomani's back as he jumped out of the passenger door, running at top speed down the street with the bag of money over his shoulder.

Bomani ran down the street at full speed, pushing people out of his way. The only thing on his mind was not getting caught. He rounded the building and made his way toward the semi-crowded platform in the back. Immediately, people began to yell and scramble to get out of the way when they saw the big assault rifle.

Bomani was just about to fire shots in the air to cause more chaos, then toss the gun and blend in with the fleeing crowd, when out of nowhere, a uniformed officer appeared in front of him.

"Freeze! Drop your weap—"

Without a second's hesitation, Bomani raised the M4 and squeezed the trigger. The vicious three-round bursts walked bullets up the officer's body, ripping through his vest as if it were a plain shirt. Bomani dropped the weapon as he spun on his heels while simultaneously drawing his Glock and hightailing it in the opposite direction.

Chapter 37

Detective Lont glanced down at the speedometer and saw that she was driving close to 100 mph. She knew she shouldn't push the unmarked MPD-issued Dodge Charger much faster, but when the car she was chasing turned into the narrow alleyway, her adrenaline kicked up, and she instinctively pressed a little harder on the accelerator.

When she rocketed out of the other end of the alley, a city bus was just pulling away from a bus stop right there. The sudden sight of the big bus startled her, nearly causing her to lose control of the car, but she recovered quickly. The loud crash that came moments behind her told her that one of the backup squad cars wasn't so lucky.

Back in the midst of city traffic, Lont slowed down a bit but not much. She skidded around the last corner she'd seen the Audi round and spotted one of the suspects jumping from the car, armed with an assault rifle, and fleeing southbound on foot. Normally, in this type of situation, she would have continued after the car, but since she knew the driver was their CI, she slammed on the brakes, jumped out of the car, drew her weapon, and took off on foot after the runner, leaving the uniformed officer riding with her to deal with the CI.

The detective knew that a desperate, heavily armed suspect running down a street filled with innocent people was a major danger that she had to stop before the fear in her gut became reality.

***

Everything about the robbery taking place before Jaheim screamed to him that it was Sentrice and the others. A smile teased his lips at seeing his girl in action, but his admiration didn't stop him from reflexively drawing his gun and ducking behind the dashboard when Bomani shot into the SUV he was in. Seeing the bullets rip through the seat beside him for a second time made the thug's heart skip a beat, but it also told him that the gunman wasn't trying to kill him. He recognized from the man's build that the masked man was Sentrice's brother. The fact that he was still breathing told Jaheim that Bomani was sending him a message to stand down.

Jaheim had every intention of doing just that, but then he saw a small fleet of squad cars chasing after the car Bomani had gotten into. Without thinking, Jaheim threw the truck into drive and shot off after them.

The big Cadillac SUV was no match for the speeding cars that had a nice head start on him, so he had to rely on his criminal instincts—which were a little off because his mind was on Sentrice. When Jaheim saw the Audi, followed by the police, turn down the alley, he didn't follow. Instead, he rounded the block, hoping he wouldn't lose them by doing so. The sight of the mangled police car pointed him in the right direction.

Jaheim rounded the next corner just in time to see who he believed to be Bomani flee from the Audi, with a female detective jumping out of an unmarked car behind the Audi and taking off running after him. Jaheim saw they were heading toward the Greyhound/Amtrak station, which is where he would go if he were the one being chased by the police. So he spun the truck around and headed toward the station.

By the time he made it there, the sound of heavy gunfire gave him a general direction to head toward. Gun in hand, Jaheim raced toward the sound of the gunfire. He ran through the hysterical rush of distraught pedestrians, all of whom were trying to put distance between themselves and the man with the big gun.

***

Lont hastily crossed the lobby of the transit station just a split second too late. Without pausing in her stride, she witnessed through one of the windows as one of her own was being mercilessly gunned down by her fleeing assailant.

"Officer down! Officer down on the southwest platform of the station. Plainclothes detective on scene and in pursuit of the armed gunman," she radioed into dispatch, already knowing from the look on the station's security officers that there was nothing she could do for her fellow officer except catch the man who killed him.

"He went that way! That way!" a distraught group of witnesses exclaimed in unison after overhearing the detective calling in the shooting.

Lont ran off in the direction the station employees and civilians were pointing her toward. She pushed through a set of heavy glass doors and, right away, spotted a man with a handgun running eastbound along the side of the tracks.

Lont instantly recalled seeing one of the security guards holding an assault rifle by its barrel—he was securing the weapon while not compromising any fingerprints that might be on it. Taking a deep breath, Lont quickly took off in a full sprint after the alleged assailant. She didn't slow down until she heard more gunfire not far from her current position. So she reduced her pace to a cautious jog and continued her approach.

Soon, Lont came upon an open gate with a heavy chain and broken lock hanging off it. She knew it was likely the reason for the gunfire she'd just heard. Expecting a fight, she extended her gun out in front of her in one hand, and with the other, she pulled the gate open and eased forward.

"Drop the gun!" she ordered with authority, now holding her gun in a two-handed grip on the armed man. "I said drop that motherfucking gun now! I have my weapon aimed at the back of your head. Don't make me use deadly force!"

She saw that the man didn't budge. He just stood there, as if weighing his options.

"Don't do it. Just please, slowly toss the gun and get on your knees!"

The suspect did as he was told. He tossed the gun to the left of him and slowly got down on his knees. He waited until the detective grabbed his wrist, then—moving in a blur—he sent a hard elbow crashing into her legs, followed by another that smashed into her hip.

Lont grunted and buckled but didn't let go of his wrist. Using the butt of her gun like a hammer, she clobbered her attacker with it, knowing she was fighting for her life. The fight didn't last long. Lont's gun caught the man in the perfect spot on the back of his head, instantly dazing him. This gave her the time she needed to slap handcuffs on him and catch her breath.

***

"Detective, are you alright?" a uniformed officer asked after rushing over and relieving Lont of the battered, bloody, cuffed suspect.

"I'm good," she claimed as she limped over to an ambulance and asked the EMTs to check out her wrist, which had gotten hurt in the fight.

"It's not broken, just a little bruised. I'll wrap it and give you an ice pack. You should be back to yourself in a day or so," the kind EMT told her, then went right to work patching her up.

"Is that the guy that did this to you?"

"Yeah and no. That's the guy I hurt my wrist on while doing this to him," Lont answered the EMT.

Once they were done with her, Lont got up and headed straight to her captain, who'd just arrived late to the scene, dressed like he was going to a ball.

"Tonya, I'm sorry to tell you this, but Detective Hermon was shot and killed in pursuit of your robbery suspects," the captain informed her.

"Oh my God. Please tell me that you got the bastard that did it?"

"Sorry, they got away," he sullenly answered. "So did the driver of the car you were chasing, due to the officer down call that came in."

"Ohh, I'm not worried about him. He's the CI, and we've got GPS on him. So if we're done here, I'd like a team so I can go round up him and the rest of his buddies now," Lont said with a confidence about herself that the captain couldn't ignore.

Chapter 38

All the way to the police station, Jaheim racked his brain trying to come up with a scheme that would justify his reason for attacking the detective. The only thing he could think of was that she had failed to identify herself as police. Since she was dressed in plain clothes and he was chasing after a man who had just robbed and killed his friends, he didn't know if she was with him or not until she put the cuffs on his wrists. Jaheim knew that the bullet-riddled SUV parked outside of the transit station would help him sell his story as well as place him at the scene of the robbery and shooting at the carwash. He couldn't think of anything better, but he knew it was best to allow a lawyer to speak on his behalf if he wanted to see daylight as a free man again. He slumped back in the seat and stared at freedom through the port-side window of the squad car. Shaking his head in disgust at his current position, Jaheim made up his mind not to say a word to anyone outside of giving them his name and date of birth during the booking process.

At the jail, he was rushed through the booking room and placed in a small holding cell with two other guys—one hogging the only working phone in the cell, and the other almost in tears with fear.

"Say, my guy, let me get that jack after you," Jaheim said in a polite, no-nonsense tone.

The medium-height, heavyset phone hogger turned around with a menacing look that instantly cleared up when he saw who was making the request.

"I got you, fam!" he said, knowing that he wasn't going to be able to bully him the way he was bullying the other guy.

After trying several times to reach someone on the phone to let them know where he was, Jaheim gave up and handed the phone back to the guy he got it from, receiving a cold glare from the other guy for not giving it to him instead. Jaheim shrugged his shoulders and took a seat on the opposite end of the cold concrete bench. He wasn't there to make friends, especially not with a coward.

Approximately two hours later, Jaheim was pulled out of the holding cell and placed directly in the segregation unit. The night captain thought it would be best to keep the alleged cop killer under close supervision while he awaited punishment.

"Hey, I ain't get a chance to use the phone!" Jaheim yelled through the heavy steel door to the deputy.

"You'll be allowed to make a call when they let you out for day room."

"When is that?"

"I believe you have first day room in the morning, so sometime then."

Knowing there was nothing he could say to convince the deputy to let him use the phone now, Jaheim made his bunk and laid down. The remaining hours of the night dragged on as he lay there reminiscing about his times with Sentrice and asking himself why he had sacrificed himself for her brother. When Jaheim closed his eyes, he could see Bomani's back as he ran off, leaving him to deal with the detective on his own. Jaheim wondered if Bomani had told Sentrice what he did for him—or if Bomani even knew that it was him who had gotten arrested.

***

Lont knew firsthand how dangerous attempting to arrest the crew was, from watching one of them gun down a police officer earlier to get away. Lont didn't want to see another one of her fellow officers killed, so she planned to creep up on the crew while they were in the house dividing up their take from the robbery.

Detective Lont, along with seven members of the MPD S.W.A.T. team, waited for the green light to storm the property. She sat in the back of the delivery van she had been using to surveil the CI's movements, a headset pressed tightly to her ear as she listened to the conversation going on inside the CI's home. From where she was parked, Lont could see two shadows passing by the closed blinds of the windows. She also noticed a car sitting idle across the street from the house with one person inside.

"We got someone in a dark sedan parked across from the house," she said, pointing out the suspicious car to the S.W.A.T. team leader.

"I've seen it. That's just a guy waiting on someone. He's probably waiting to go get laid," he chuckled.

Lont didn't laugh, but since he wasn't concerned about the guy in the car being a threat, she took him at his word and ignored the car as well.

After Sentrice and Shiesty switched from the stolen BMW into their own vehicles and parted ways, knowing where to meet back up, Shiesty received a call from Bomani to come pick him up from where he was hiding on the outside deck of a restaurant. Once they were together, Bomani filled him in on all that had happened and told him that both he and Sentrice believed DB was working with the police to bring them down.

"Bo, I was gonna bring that up to you that day I got into the fight at yo' crib, but that shit had me thrown off. Anyway, my bitch told me she'd seen DB in a shootout with the police.

She said they shot out his tire and that's why he crashed. Man, I didn't believe the shit, that's why I didn't bring it back up," Shiesty admitted when Bomani finished filling him in.

"It's all good, bro. I didn't wanna believe it either, but after today I have to. I'ma kill the nigga myself if he even hesitates a little when I question him about it," Bomani said, resting his head back on the headrest of the car seat. "Take me to his crib. That's where I told him to meet me at after we split up."

As they headed over to DB's house, they both thought of all the times they'd been there for DB over the years. It hurt them hearing that someone they called family had betrayed them.

"You want me to holla at him?" Shiesty asked when he pulled up in front of DB's place and parked.

"Nah, I'll be back in a second," Bomani answered, then got out of the car and briskly strolled up to the house and went inside.

Shiesty sat behind the wheel of his car, watching the surroundings and texting on his phone. He was just about to switch to a game when he caught movement on the side of the house. Looking closer, he saw that it was police trying to creep.

"Shit, shit, shit!" he cursed, grabbing his modified fully automatic Glock 40 off the seat beside him where he'd placed it when Bomani got out of the car. Then he hopped out.

***

After a few minutes, the chatter the detective was listening to turned angry, and afterward, she heard and saw flashes of gunfire.

"Come on, we have to move now!" she bellowed, tossing off the headphones and pushing her way out of the van.

Lont, along with the S.W.A.T. members, instantly jumped out of the delivery van and moved to surround the threat. They were just about in position when, out of nowhere, the man from the car started shooting at them. Lont watched as two members of S.W.A.T. were gunned down. She quickly dived behind a parked car for cover as bullets ricocheted off the ground and across the cars around her.

The skillful S.W.A.T. team returned fire in the direction of the gunman, turning the ambush into a shootout.

Shiesty quickly ran to the other side of the car and ducked when the police returned fire. He popped up from behind his car and fired some more when a bullet ripped through his arm and shoulder, causing him to drop down to the ground. He looked and saw his blood everywhere. He immediately felt like he was going to die, so he reached for his gun with his good hand, planning on going out with a bang. That's when two S.W.A.T. officers suddenly appeared and put several hot slugs in his chest, killing him instantly.

Chapter 39

The sudden sound of gunfire startled the emotionally charged men. Bomani dashed across the room and peeked out of the front window. What he saw was one of his greatest fears manifesting right before his eyes. He watched his loyal partner and friend locked in a deadly gun battle with a S.W.A.T. team that had him pinned behind his car. Bomani's anger instantly rocketed to ten when he realized that everything was true about DB.

"What's happening? What's going on?" DB inquired, his voice cracky and full of fear.

"Bitch-ass nigga, we ain't finna do this! You know what's going on! What kinda nigga sets up his friends? Fuck that—his family?"

"What? Whoa, Bo, you're trippin' right now. I would never do no shit like that," he lied, taking nervous steps backward away from the window and Bomani.

"Trippin'? Fuck you!" Bomani barked. With a broken heart, he raised his gun and shook his head in disappointment as he squeezed the trigger. Killing DB was like losing a piece of himself, but it was clear—just as the unfair gun battle outside the house—that it was DB who said "fuck them" first. DB had killed himself when he chose to become a snitch, and even more so by doing it to the ones he so-called loved.

Bomani glanced out the window again. This time, he saw that the police were focused on Shiesty and not the house.

161

He knew that his window for escape was narrow, and he had to go for it or die trying. Running through the house and out the back door, Bomani crouched and jogged across the dark yard, hiding behind DB's prized 2018 souped-up Dodge Challenger. That's when he saw a set of officers taking cover in the gangway beside DB's place.

Right away, his mind started looking for the best escape route. That's when he remembered that DB kept a spare key to the car in a magnetic box inside the rear quarter panel—just in case he ever found himself in a predicament like the one he'd put Bomani and Shiesty in now. Bomani grabbed the key and eased inside the car. Not wanting to alert the police, he snatched the gear shifter into neutral and pushed it out into the alley, letting it roll down the slight slope of the alley.

When he heard the shooting stop, he knew Shiesty was no longer alive. It hurt him to have to leave him like that, but he knew Shiesty had sacrificed himself so that he could get away, and he wasn't about to let his friend's sacrifice be for nothing. At the end of the alley, Bomani started the car and calmly drove away from the scene.

***

Lont gave the order for them to breach the house, then she followed three of the heavily armed men inside. Right away, they fanned out and searched the place. In the living room, she found DB lying lifeless on his back. The informant had been shot in the face at close range. Lont cut her eyes away from the gruesome mess.

Her team cleared the house and reported no sign of any other suspects. She was disappointed she didn't catch her last man, but knowing that three of the four outlaws were dead or behind bars gave her a little comfort.

On her way out, she thought she saw movement creeping around in the dark alley, so she took off to check it out. But when she got there, it was empty, and there was nothing noticeable to show anyone had been there. The only thing she saw was a set of taillights that didn't spark her suspicion. Lont had to face the fact that her other suspect was long gone.

***

Anxiously, Sentrice paced back and forth, her cellphone in one hand tapping it against her thigh and a stiff drink in the other. She had made it home over an hour ago after splitting up with Shiesty, not long after they'd successfully evaded capture when she shot the detective following them. Now, she felt like something was wrong because neither Shiesty nor Bomani had made it there or contacted her.

Knowing that DB was working with the police, all the waiting made Sentrice's thoughts race to dark places. She didn't want to think the worst, but having a snitch in their mix made it real hard not to—especially knowing that neither one of the men she was expecting would be caught without putting up a fight.

Sentrice tried to calm herself by thinking of Jaheim. She went over to the table and picked up his cellphone to see if she recognized any of the missed calls or texts on it. It made her smile to see her photo pop up on his home screen. She didn't recognize any of the numbers, but there were a few from his cousin LaQuess.

Sentrice's first thought was that it was Jaheim calling from his cousin's phone, trying to find his phone, so she sent a text back telling LaQuess that Jaheim had left his phone at her house and to tell him that she really needed to talk to him—so to just come over as soon as possible.

A short time later, the phone rang, displaying LaQuess's number, so Sentrice answered it. LaQuess told her that she was looking for Jaheim herself because his car had been sitting in a gas station lot all day, and it had her worried. They both agreed to call one another if they heard from him.

Now, with Jaheim missing, Sentrice had more to worry about. She was just about to break one of Bomani's top five rules by calling him when she suddenly heard banging at her back door. She rushed to open it.

"What the hell, Bo! I was so fuckin' worried that I was just about to call and check up on you," she exclaimed as he rushed into the house. "And why are you so damn dirty?"

"Man, damn, Sis, it's been crazy," he began, taking the drink from her and emptying the glass in one swallow. "The police got behind us, and I could tell that DB wasn't trying to lose 'em, so I split up with him. Just like I thought, the police came after me instead of him in the car. I had to drop one of 'em that tried to corner me. The only reason I got away is because of your boyfriend showing up."

"Jaheim?"

"Yeah, who else would I be talkin' about? I think they got him, though. I heard shooting, and when I looked behind me, he was just standing there. I couldn't see nothing, but I think the police had him at gunpoint. That's the only reason I can think of why he would've froze like that."

"That's fuckin' crazy. His cousin just called me and said that his car is parked in a gas station. So, Bo, what in the fuck did you do, for real? Why was he—"

"Sen, I didn't do shit to him. On Mom and Dad, I didn't! The nigga was in one of the trucks we hit. I sent warning shots for him to stand down, that's it. I guess he came after me for doing it. Maybe he was looking for you, I don't know, but I didn't do shit to him," Bomani said, walking into the other room to refill the glass.

"Arggrrh! Let me text his cousin and tell her to look for him in the county," she said, forcing herself to believe her brother as her fingers blazed across the screen of the phone. "Where is Shiesty? Have you heard from him?"

"Ah, Sen, bro didn't make it. I called him to come get me, then I had him take me to handle DB's rat ass. The nigga DB had the police waiting on us because, right after we got there to handle him, they came. Shiesty got into a shootout with them. That's how I got away. It took me so long to get here because I didn't want to leave him out there stranded if he had somehow gotten himself outta that jam. But when I saw a body laid out beside his car . . ." Bomani fell silent and just shook his head. "I should've helped him, but it was way too many of them, and I had to get back to you."

"Oh my God, no!" Sentrice exclaimed in shock at what she was hearing. "No, no, no! This is some bullshit!"

"Sen, we gotta get outta here. We gotta do it now. I don't know what all DB told the police about us or what they got on us. I do know that we'll have a better chance if we're not in this state."

"Bo, I don't wanna leave without Jaheim."

"Sen, you have to. I know it's what he would want because the nigga loves you enough to marry you. We gotta go, and I promise I'll work on helping him if I can."

Reluctantly, Sentrice agreed. They packed the money she'd gotten away with in her car and hit the road, heading to Florida because it was the only safe place they could think of.

EPILOGUE

"Black! Black? Wakey wakey!" called the female deputy through the intercom in the cell, pulling Jaheim awake.

"Yeah . . . yeah," he answered groggily, disappointed that the voice he was hearing in his sleep didn't belong to the woman of his dreams.

"Step over to the cell door so I can see you, please?"

Jaheim got up and dragged himself over to the door to see what the deputy wanted with him so early in the morning. He was really mad at her for waking him because he had been helping her through her night shift by holding friendly conversations with her over the past few nights. After sitting three weeks in jail with no bond on the segregation block—which eventually emptied out, leaving him the only inmate in his block—they used one another for entertainment.

"What you on? I was on an island somewhere sunny. Hater!" he joked, looking at her through the half-inch ballistic glass of the cell door. The same safety glass enclosed the front wall of the cell block.

"If I gotta be here, then so do you," she giggled. "I'm not a hater like that. I wouldn't wake you for nothing. You have court this morning—they just called me and told me to have you ready."

"Court? You sure you got the right person? I don't have court until next week," Jaheim explained, losing the grogginess in his voice.

"Yeah, I'm sure. Transport will be here soon, so get ready."

Jaheim knew that, in most cases, sudden court dates were usually a bad sign. A little fearful and curious, he paced the small holding cell, sipping on the milk from his breakfast bag that the transport deputy gave him when he came for him. Jaheim caught a glimpse of two Feds standing at the officer's station and instantly lost his appetite. Not long after seeing the Feds, his cell door was popped, and he was once again handcuffed—only this time, they added shackles to his feet for added security.

When he entered the courtroom, the first thing he did was search the tables for the federal agents. Jaheim breathed a sigh of relief when he didn't see them in the courtroom. Feeling a little eased, he scanned the small crowd of onlookers for anyone he knew. He spotted LaQuess and her mother right away and got a surprise when he saw Sentrice standing right beside them. He flashed a smile, then took his seat beside a lawyer he didn't know.

"Good morning, Jaheim. My name is Rosenberg," the lawyer introduced himself, giving Jaheim an elbow bump in place of a handshake. "I've been hired to represent you today. I do apologize for not coming to see you before now. Well, let me ask you before I continue—are you okay with me representing you?"

"Yeah, as long as you know what you're doing. I don't even know why I'm in court today. I'm not supposed to have it until next week," Jaheim answered and explained, unable to stop glancing back over his shoulder at Sentrice.

"Okay, good. But you're going to need to keep your eyes forward when the judge takes his seat. We don't need to upset him. Real quick: if you agree to taking a plea for the gun today, I believe I can get this taken care of for you," Rosenberg said, sliding the paperwork that Jaheim needed to sign in front of him.

"How much time do they want outta me?"

"Good question. The state is asking for nine months in and a year probation."

"Yeah, right. What about me fighting with the police? Are you saying that they just gonna forget about that?"

"No, but as you pointed out to your last attorney, you didn't know that it was a plainclothes officer at the time because the officer failed to announce herself as such. Thanks to the body cam, your story checks out."

"Okay, alright, I know how this goes. Just so you know, if I see this going sideways, I'ma fire you right here and right now," Jaheim told him.

A short time after Jaheim had signed the paperwork, a cranky-looking judge came in and took his seat on the bench.

"State of Wisconsin versus Jaheim Black," the court's secretary announced.

After all the greetings and instructions were given, the ADA sorted through a file folder. When he found what he needed, he addressed the courtroom.

"Your Honor, I see no point in dragging this out this morning. After my investigation of the information, the State sees no reason to pursue the charge of battery to an officer against Mr. Black, and moves this court to dismiss. Mr. Black has signed an agreement admitting guilt for the possession and unlawful discharge of a firearm. For this, the State asks that the court impose nine months of incarceration and twelve months of probation, as stated in the agreement."

"Mr. Black, do you understand these terms and that I do not have to go along with them?" the judge asked.

"Yes," Jaheim answered.

"Do you agree to the terms, knowing that I can sentence you to any amount of time that I see fit for the charges you're agreeing to?" Again, Jaheim answered yes.

"Okay, Mr. Black, this court accepts that you understand what you've signed. In light of the pandemic, I'm going to impose this as a stayed sentence. This means that if you catch another charge within the probation, you will not only have to serve the time for the new case, but also the nine months that you've agreed to here today," the judge ordered with a finalizing drop of his gavel.

When Jaheim was being led out of the courtroom, Sentrice stood up, waving to get his attention. Once she had it, she showed him that she had on the ring he'd left for her, and with a smile, she mouthed the words, "I love you."

Jaheim looked back at the lawyer and knew that he was walking out of there because of Sentrice.

"I love you more!" he shouted back to her, then was escorted out of the room to be released.

THE END

Lock Down Publications and Ca$h Presents
Assisted Publishing Packages

Due to an increase in the price of services we have increased our prices. The prices below reflect the price increase as of 11/1/24.

BASIC PACKAGE **$699** Editing Cover Design Formatting	UPGRADED PACKAGE **$1000** Typing Editing Cover Design Formatting Upload eBooks to Amazon Upload Paperback to Amazon
ADVANCE PACKAGE **$1,400** Typing Editing (line editing/content) Cover Design Formatting Copyright Registration Proofreading Upload eBooks to Amazon Upload Paperback to Amazon	LDP SUPREME PACKAGE **$1,700** Typing Editing (line editing/content) Cover Design Formatting Copyright Registration Proofreading Set up Amazon Account Upload eBooks to Amazon Upload Paperback to Amazon Advertise on LDP's Amazon and Facebook Page

***Other services available upon request.
Additional charges may apply

Lock Down Publications
P.O. Box 944
Stockbridge, GA 30281-9998
Phone: 470 303-9761
Email: lockdownpublications@gmail.com

Submission Guideline

Submit the first three chapters of your completed manuscript to ldpsubmissions@gmail.com. In the subject line add **Your Book's Title**. The manuscript must be in a Word Doc file and sent as an attachment. Document should be in Times New Roman, double spaced, and in size 12 font. Also, provide your synopsis and full contact information. If sending multiple submissions, they must each be in a separate email.

Have a story but no way to send it electronically? You can still submit to LDP/Ca$h Presents. Send in the first three chapters, written or typed, of your completed manuscript to:

LDP: Submissions Dept
P.O. Box 944
Stockbridge, GA 30281-9998

DO NOT send original manuscript. Must be a duplicate.
Provide your synopsis and a cover letter containing your full contact information.

Thanks for considering LDP and Ca$h Presents.

NEW RELEASES

BLOODLINE OF A SAVAGE 1&2
THESE VICIOUS STREETS 1&2
RELENTLESS GOON
RELENTLESS GOON 2
BY PRINCE A. TAUHID

THE BUTTERFLY MAFIA 1-3
BY FUMIYA PAYNE

A THUG'S STREET PRINCESS 1&2
BY MEESHA

CITY OF SMOKE 2
BY MOLOTTI

STEPPERS 1,2&3
THE REAL BADDIES OF CHI-RAQ
BY KING RIO

THE LANE 1&2
BY KEN-KEN SPENCE

THUG OF SPADES 1&2
LOVE IN THE TRENCHES 2
CORNER BOYS
BY COREY ROBINSON

TIL DEATH 3
BY ARYANNA

THE BIRTH OF A GANGSTER 4
BY DELMONT PLAYER

PRODUCT OF THE STREETS 1&2
BY DEMOND "MONEY" ANDERSON

NO TIME FOR ERROR
BY KEESE

MONEY HUNGRY DEMONS
BY TRANAY ADAMS

Coming Soon from Lock Down Publications/Ca$h Presents

IF YOU CROSS ME ONCE 6
ANGEL V
By Anthony Fields

IMMA DIE BOUT MINE 5
By Aryanna

A THUGS STREET PRINCESS 3
By Meesha

PRODUCT OF THE STREETS 3
By Demond Money Anderson

CORNER BOYS 2
By Corey Robinson

THE MURDER QUEENS 6&7
By Michael Gallon

CITY OF SMOKE 3
By Molotti

CONFESSIONS OF A DOPE BOY
By Nicholas Lock

THA TAKEOVER
By Keith Chandler

BETRAYAL OF A G 2
By Ray Vinci

CRIME BOSS
By Playa Ray

Available Now

RESTRAINING ORDER 1 & 2
By **CA$H & Coffee**

LOVE KNOWS NO BOUNDARIES 1-3
By **Coffee**

RAISED AS A GOON I, II, III & IV
BRED BY THE SLUMS I, II, III
BLAST FOR ME I & II
ROTTEN TO THE CORE I II III
A BRONX TALE I, II, III
DUFFLE BAG CARTEL I II III IV V VI
HEARTLESS GOON I II III IV V
A SAVAGE DOPEBOY I II
DRUG LORDS I II III
CUTTHROAT MAFIA I II
KING OF THE TRENCHES
By **Ghost**

LAY IT DOWN I & II
LAST OF A DYING BREED I II
BLOOD STAINS OF A SHOTTA I & II III
By **Jamaica**

LOYAL TO THE GAME I II III
LIFE OF SIN I, II III
By **TJ & Jelissa**

IF LOVING HIM IS WRONG...I & II
LOVE ME EVEN WHEN IT HURTS I II III
By **Jelissa**

PUSH IT TO THE LIMIT
By **Bre' Hayes**

BLOODY COMMAS I & II
SKI MASK CARTEL I, II & III
KING OF NEW YORK I II, III IV V
RISE TO POWER I II III
COKE KINGS I II III IV V
BORN HEARTLESS I II III IV
KING OF THE TRAP I II
By **T.J. Edwards**

WHEN THE STREETS CLAP BACK I & II III
THE HEART OF A SAVAGE I II III IV
MONEY MAFIA I II
LOYAL TO THE SOIL I II III
By **Jibril Williams**

A DISTINGUISHED THUG STOLE MY HEART I II & III
LOVE SHOULDN'T HURT I II III IV
RENEGADE BOYS 1-4
PAID IN KARMA 1-3
SAVAGE STORMS 1-3
AN UNFORESEEN LOVE 1-3
BABY, I'M WINTERTIME COLD 1-3
A THUG'S STREET PRINCESS 1&2
By **Meesha**

A GANGSTER'S CODE 1-3
A GANGSTER'S SYN 1-3
THE SAVAGE LIFE 1-3
CHAINED TO THE STREETS 1-3
BLOOD ON THE MONEY 1-3
A GANGSTA'S PAIN 1-3
BEAUTIFUL LIES AND UGLY TRUTHS
CHURCH IN THESE STREETS
By **J-Blunt**

CUM FOR ME 1-8
An LDP Erotica Collaboration

BLOOD OF A BOSS 1-5
SHADOWS OF THE GAME
TRAP BASTARD
By **Askari**

THE STREETS BLEED MURDER 1-3
THE HEART OF A GANGSTA 1-3
By **Jerry Jackson**

WHEN A GOOD GIRL GOES BAD
By **Adrienne**

THE COST OF LOYALTY 1-3
By **Kweli**

BRIDE OF A HUSTLA 1-3
THE FETTI GIRLS 1-3
CORRUPTED BY A GANGSTA 1-4
BLINDED BY HIS LOVE
THE PRICE YOU PAY FOR LOVE 1-3
DOPE GIRL MAGIC 1-3
By **Destiny Skai**

A KINGPIN'S AMBITION
A KINGPIN'S AMBITION II
I MURDER FOR THE DOUGH
By **Ambitious**

TRUE SAVAGE 1-7
DOPE BOY MAGIC 1-3
MIDNIGHT CARTEL 1-3
CITY OF KINGZ 1&2
NIGHTMARE ON SILENT AVE
THE PLUG OF LIL MEXICO 1&2
CLASSIC CITY
By **Chris Green**

A GANGSTER'S REVENGE 1-4
THE BOSS MAN'S DAUGHTERS 1-5
A SAVAGE LOVE 1&2
BAE BELONGS TO ME 1&2
A HUSTLER'S DECEIT 1-3
WHAT BAD BITCHES DO 1-3
SOUL OF A MONSTER 1-3
KILL ZONE
A DOPE BOY'S QUEEN 1-3
TIL DEATH 1-3
IMMA DIE BOUT MINE 1-4
By **Aryanna**

A DOPEBOY'S PRAYER
By **Eddie "Wolf" Lee**

THE KING CARTEL 1-3
By **Frank Gresham**

THESE NIGGAS AIN'T LOYAL 1-3
By **Nikki Tee**

GANGSTA SHYT 1-3
By **CATO**

THE ULTIMATE BETRAYAL
By **Phoenix**

BOSS'N UP 1-3
By **Royal Nicole**

I LOVE YOU TO DEATH
By **Destiny J**

I RIDE FOR MY HITTA
I STILL RIDE FOR MY HITTA
By **Misty Holt**

LOVE & CHASIN' PAPER
By **Qay Crockett**

TO DIE IN VAIN
SINS OF A HUSTLA
By **ASAD**

BROOKLYN HUSTLAZ
By **Boogsy Morina**

BROOKLYN ON LOCK 1 & 2
By **Sonovia**

GANGSTA CITY
By **Teddy Duke**

A DRUG KING AND HIS DIAMOND 1-3
A DOPEMAN'S RICHES
HER MAN, MINE'S TOO 1&2
CASH MONEY HO'S
THE WIFEY I USED TO BE 1&2
PRETTY GIRLS DO NASTY THINGS
By **Nicole Goosby**

LIPSTICK KILLAH 1-3
CRIME OF PASSION 1-3
FRIEND OR FOE 1-3
By **Mimi**

TRAPHOUSE KING 1-3
KINGPIN KILLAZ 1-3
STREET KINGS 1&2
PAID IN BLOOD 1&2
CARTEL KILLAZ 1-3
DOPE GODS 1&2
By **Hood Rich**

THE STREETS ARE CALLING
By **Duquie Wilson**

STEADY MOBBN' 1-3
THE STREETS STAINED MY SOUL 1-3
By **Marcellus Allen**

WHO SHOT YA 1-3
SON OF A DOPE FIEND 1-4
HEAVEN GOT A GHETTO 1&2
SKI MASK MONEY 1&2
By **Renta**

GORILLAZ IN THE BAY 1-4
TEARS OF A GANGSTA 1/&2
3X KRAZY 1&2
STRAIGHT BEAST MODE 1&2
By **DE'KARI**

TRIGGADALE 1-3
MURDA WAS THE CASE 1-3
By **Elijah R. Freeman**

SLAUGHTER GANG 1-3
RUTHLESS HEART 1-3
By **Willie Slaughter**

GOD BLESS THE TRAPPERS 1-3
THESE SCANDALOUS STREETS 1-3
FEAR MY GANGSTA 1-5
THESE STREETS DON'T LOVE NOBODY 1-2
BURY ME A G 1-5
A GANGSTA'S EMPIRE 1-4
THE DOPEMAN'S BODYGAURD 1&2
THE REALEST KILLAZ 1-3
THE LAST OF THE OGS 1-3
By **Tranay Adams**

MARRIED TO A BOSS 1-3
By **Destiny Skai & Chris Green**

KINGZ OF THE GAME 1-7
CRIME BOSS 1-3
By **Playa Ray**

FUK SHYT
By **Blakk Diamond**

DON'T F#CK WITH MY HEART 1&2
By **Linnea**

ADDICTED TO THE DRAMA 1-3
IN THE ARM OF HIS BOSS
By **Jamila**

LOYALTY AIN'T PROMISED 1&2
By **Keith Williams**

YAYO 1-4
A SHOOTER'S AMBITION 1&2
BRED IN THE GAME
By **S. Allen**

TRAP GOD 1-3
RICH $AVAGE 1-3
MONEY IN THE GRAVE 1-3
CARTEL MONEY
By **Martell Troublesome Bolden**

FOREVER GANGSTA 1&2
GLOCKS ON SATIN SHEETS 1&2
By **Adrian Dulan**

TOE TAGZ 1-4
LEVELS TO THIS SHYT 1&2
IT'S JUST ME AND YOU
By **Ah'Million**

KINGPIN DREAMS 1-3
RAN OFF ON DA PLUG
By **Paper Boi Rari**

THE STREETS MADE ME 1-3
By **Larry D. Wright**

CONFESSIONS OF A GANGSTA 1-4
CONFESSIONS OF A JACKBOY 1-3
CONFESSIONS OF A HITMAN
By **Nicholas Lock**

I'M NOTHING WITHOUT HIS LOVE
SINS OF A THUG
TO THE THUG I LOVED BEFORE
A GANGSTA SAVED XMAS
IN A HUSTLER I TRUST
By **Monet Dragun**

QUIET MONEY 1-3
THUG LIFE 1-3
EXTENDED CLIP 1&2
A GANGSTA'S PARADISE
By **Trai'Quan**

CAUGHT UP IN THE LIFE 1-3
THE STREETS NEVER LET GO 1-3
By **Robert Baptiste**

NEW TO THE GAME 1-3
MONEY, MURDER & MEMORIES 1-3
By **Malik D. Rice**

CREAM 2-3
THE STREETS WILL TALK
By **Yolanda Moore**

THE STREETS WILL NEVER CLOSE 1-3
By **K'ajji**

LIFE OF A SAVAGE 1-4
A GANGSTA'S QUR'AN 1-4
MURDA SEASON 1-3
GANGLAND CARTEL 1-3
CHI'RAQ GANGSTAS 1-4
KILLERS ON ELM STREET 1-3
JACK BOYZ N DA BRONX 1-3
A DOPEBOY'S DREAM 1-3
JACK BOYS VS DOPE BOYS 1-3
COKE GIRLZ
COKE BOYS
SOSA GANG 1&2
BRONX SAVAGES
BODYMORE KINGPINS
BLOOD OF A GOON
By **Romell Tukes**

CONCRETE KILLA 1-3
VICIOUS LOYALTY 1-3
By **Kingpen**

THE ULTIMATE SACRIFICE 1-6
KHADIFI
IF YOU CROSS ME ONCE 1-3
ANGEL 1-4
IN THE BLINK OF AN EYE
By **Anthony Fields**

THE LIFE OF A HOOD STAR
By **Ca$h & Rashia Wilson**

NIGHTMARES OF A HUSTLA 1-3
BLOOD AND GAMES 1&2
By **King Dream**

GHOST MOB
By **Stilloan Robinson**

HARD AND RUTHLESS 1&2
MOB TOWN 251
THE BILLIONAIRE BENTLEYS 1-3
REAL G'S MOVE IN SILENCE
By **Von Diesel**

MOB TIES 1-7
SOUL OF A HUSTLER, HEART OF A KILLER 1-3
GORILLAZ IN THE TRENCHES
By **SayNoMore**

BODYMORE MURDERLAND 1-3
THE BIRTH OF A GANGSTER 1-4
By **Delmont Player**

FOR THE LOVE OF A BOSS 1&2
By **C. D. Blue**

KILLA KOUNTY 1-5
By **Khufu**

MOBBED UP 1-4
THE BRICK MAN 1-5
THE COCAINE PRINCESS 1-10
STEPPERS 1-3
SUPER GREMLIN 1-4
By **King Rio**

MONEY GAME 1&2
By **Smoove Dolla**

A GANGSTA'S KARMA 1-4
By **FLAME**

KING OF THE TRENCHES 1-3
By **GHOST & TRANAY ADAMS**

QUEEN OF THE ZOO 1&2
By **Black Migo**

GRIMEY WAYS 1-3
BETRAYAL OF A G
By **Ray Vinci**

XMAS WITH AN ATL SHOOTER
By **Ca$h & Destiny Skai**

KING KILLA 1&2
By **Vincent "Vitto" Holloway**

BETRAYAL OF A THUG 1&2
By **Fre$h**

THE MURDER QUEENS 1-5
By **Michael Gallon**

FOR THE LOVE OF BLOOD 1-4
By **Jamel Mitchell**

HOOD CONSIGLIERE 1&2
NO TIME FOR ERROR
By **Keese**

PROTÉGÉ OF A LEGEND 1&2
LOVE IN THE TRENCHES 1&2
By **Corey Robinson**

THE PLUG'S RUTHLESS DAUGHTER
By **Tony Daniels**

BORN IN THE GRAVE 1-3
CRIME PAYS
By **Self Made Tay**

MOAN IN MY MOUTH
By **XTASY**

TORN BETWEEN A GANGSTER AND A GENTLEMAN
By **J-BLUNT & Miss Kim**

LOYALTY IS EVERYTHING 1-3
CITY OF SMOKE 1&2
By **Molotti**

HERE TODAY GONE TOMORROW 1&2
By **Fly Rock**

WOMEN LIE MEN LIE 1-4
FIFTY SHADES OF SNOW 1-3
STACK BEFORE YOU SPLURGE
GIRLS FALL LIKE DOMINOES
NAÏVE TO THE STREETS
By **ROY MILLIGAN**

PILLOW PRINCESS
By **S. Hawkins**

THE BUTTERFLY MAFIA 1-3
SALUTE MY SAVAGERY 1&2
By **Fumiya Payne**

THE LANE 1&2
By Ken-Ken Spence

THE PUSSY TRAP 1-5
By **Nene Capri**

DIRTY DNA
By **Blaque**

SANCTIFIED AND HORNY
by **XTASY**

BOOKS BY LDP'S CEO, CA$H

TRUST IN NO MAN
TRUST IN NO MAN 2
TRUST IN NO MAN 3
BONDED BY BLOOD
SHORTY GOT A THUG
THUGS CRY
THUGS CRY 2
THUGS CRY 3
TRUST NO BITCH
TRUST NO BITCH 2
TRUST NO BITCH 3
TIL MY CASKET DROPS
RESTRAINING ORDER
RESTRAINING ORDER 2
IN LOVE WITH A CONVICT
LIFE OF A HOOD STAR
XMAS WITH AN ATL SHOOTER